Of Courage Undaunted

Also by James Daugherty

ABRAHAM LINCOLN

ANDY AND THE LION

DANIEL BOONE

MARCUS AND NARCISSA WHITMAN, PIONEERS OF OREGON

POOR RICHARD

THE MAGNA CHARTA

OF COURAGE UNDAUNTED

Across the Continent with Lewis and Clark

BY

JAMES DAUGHERTY

BEAUTIFUL FEET BOOKS

Printed in the United States of America.
Library of Congress Control Number: 2008937964
ISBN 978-1-893103-02-3

Beautiful Feet Books
1306 Mill Street
San Luis Obispo, CA 93401
www.bfbooks.com
800.889.1978

To My Brother

William Telfair Daugherty

for

Courage, Loyalty and Affection

Of Meriwether Lewis

OF COURAGE UNDAUNTED;

POSSESSING A FIRMNESS OF PURPOSE WHICH NOTHING BUT IMPOSSIBILITIES COULD DIVERT FROM ITS DIRECTION;

CAREFUL AS A FATHER OF THOSE COMMITTED TO HIS CHARGE,

YET STEADY IN THE MAINTENANCE OF ORDER AND DISCIPLINE;

INTIMATE WITH THE INDIAN CHARACTER, CUSTOMS, AND PRINCIPLES;

HABITUATED TO THE HUNTING LIFE;

GUARDED BY EXACT OBSERVATION OF THE VEGETABLES AND ANIMALS OF HIS OWN COUNTRY

AGAINST LOSING TIME IN THE DESCRIPTION OF OBJECTS ALREADY POSSESSED;

HONEST, DISINTERESTED, LIBERAL, OF SOUND UNDERSTANDING AND A FIDELITY TO TRUTH SO SCRUPULOUS,

THAT WHATEVER HE SHOULD REPORT WOULD BE AS CERTAIN AS SEEN BY OURSELVES;

WITH ALL THESE QUALIFICATIONS,

AS IF SELECTED AND IMPLANTED BY NATURE IN ONE BODY FOR THIS EXPRESS PURPOSE,

I COULD HAVE NO HESITATION IN CONFIDING THE ENTERPRISE TO HIM.

Th: Jefferson

Contents

Some Persons of the Story

President Thomas Jefferson
Meriwether Lewis
William Clark
Some Members of the Corps of Discovery
- Four Sergeants: Charles Floyd, Nathaniel Pryor, John Ordway, Patrick Gass
- John Colter, a mountain man
- George Drewyer, interpreter
- Pierre Cruzatte, a riverman
- Reuben and Joseph Fields, brothers
- John Shields, a gunsmith
- George Shannon, a young adventurer
- York, Clark's Negro slave
- Toussaint Charbonneau, an interpreter
- Sacajawea, Charbonneau's Shoshone wife, called Janey
- Jean Baptiste, called Pompey, her baby
- Scannon, Lewis's Newfoundland dog

Indian Chiefs
- The Black Buffalo, a Sioux chief
- The Black Cat, a Mandan chief
- Cameahwait, chief of the Shoshones, Sacajawea's brother
- Twisted Hair, a Chopunnish Chief
- Comowool, chief of the Clatsops

Indian Tribes
- Sioux, Mandan, Shoshone, Clatsops, Chopunnish

Creatures
- Horses, buffalo, bears, beaver, wolves, birds, fleas, mosquitoes

Rivers
- Missouri, Maria's, Yellowstone, Jefferson, Columbia

Scene: America from the Potomac River to the Pacific Ocean
Time: May 14, 1804 (started up the Missouri) to September 23, 1806 (returned to St. Louis)
Distance: 3555 miles from St. Louis to the Pacific (Clark's estimate)

PART I

The Start

The Corps of Discovery

There was nothing that you would say was special about them.
They chawed tobacco and cussed and caterwauled that
they were double-jointed, fire-eating, leather-necked, half-horse
half-alligator men who could lick their weight in wildcats.
They were picked almost at random out of the Ohio Valley
of Virginia, Kentucky, Tennessee, or New England stock,
merely a sample fistful of what American democracy turns out,
as you might pick a handful of leaves and say, These are oak.

Any state in the Union can give you ten thousand such
at any time, or ten times ten thousand, if there is a call
to stand together in time of danger,
or hold the line on land, in the sea or air,
not without bragging and grousing and a sour kind of humor,
sometimes terribly scared but never
broken by fear, of courage undaunted.

Sweating and rank, coarse, muscular, lanky,
level-eyed, generous minded, free speaking, slangy—
you don't have to go far in any city or town to find them;
no farther than any street corner
or factory bench, farmyard, filling station, public high school.
As Lincoln said, "God must have loved them or
he would not have made so many."

U.S.A., MARCH 4, 1801

THE BANG of artillery thundered across the Potomac and echoed back from the Virginia hills.

Washington, D. C., the new capital of the United States, was saluting the inauguration of Thomas Jefferson.

At noon, Mr. Jefferson, with an escort of friends, had walked from Conrad's boarding house to the Capitol Building to be the chief actor in the ceremonies. As he entered the Senate Chamber, the waiting Congress stood while he seated himself in the chair which until a week ago he had occupied as Vice-President. Beside him on one side sat Chief Justice Marshall, on the other his defeated opponent, Aaron Burr. John Adams, the retiring president, had left the city at four o'clock that morning without waiting to greet the new President.

Mr. Jefferson rose from his seat, unfolding his tall frame to its full height. In a low voice he read to the silent Congress his inaugural address. At the end he said:

"We are all Republicans; we are all Federalists. If there be any among us who would wish to dissolve this Union or to change its Republican form, let them stand undisturbed as monuments of the safety with which error of opinion may be tolerated where reason is left free to combat it."

History was changing scenes in the great American drama, and the curtain was going up on a new act. Mr. Jefferson and the new democratic people's party, calling themselves Republicans, had ousted the aristocratic Federalists and their famous leader Alexander Hamilton. The people had been stirred to anger by the vicious Alien and Sedition Acts and had staged a second revolution, this time with ballots instead of bullets.

Wanted: A Secretary

Jefferson moved into the President's Mansion at the west end of Pennsylvania Avenue. His wife, his beloved Martha, had died many years ago. He would need a hostess to preside over the new household and manage its affairs. He invited sparkling Dolly Madison, the wife of his devoted friend and Secretary of State, James Madison, to become hostess at the President's Mansion. She brought the wit, easy grace, and ample hospitality of Virginia ways to the newly established household in the draughty mansion where Abigail Adams had dried the family wash in the unfinished East Room.

The President himself did away with the stuffy ceremonies

and formalities so dear to the Federalists, and got down to business. Right off he needed a personal secretary of a special sort. He did not want fancy frills but someone trustworthy and close-mouthed who was also understanding and democratic.

Himself a Virginian, he naturally thought of his beloved Charlottesville and the loyal people of Albemarle County. He remembered gallant "Mother Marks" and her coon-hunting son, Meriwether Lewis. Ten years had passed since the boy had pleaded with him to be sent on an exploring expedition across the Mississippi with the French botanist André Micheaux. Micheaux had been found to be a French secret agent and the plan had been abandoned. Jefferson learned that young Lewis was now in the United States Army.

The President wrote a letter to Commander Wilkinson, enclosing his offer to Meriwether of the post of private secretary to the President.

In the letter to Lewis, he said:

> Washington, February 3, 1801
>
> Dear Sir,
>
> The appointment to the presidency of the U.S. has rendered it necessary for me to have a private secretary, and in selecting one I have thought it important to expect not only his capacity to aid in the private concern of the household, but also to contribute to the mass of information for the administration to acquire. . . . Your knowledge of the Western country, of the army and of its interests and relations has rendered it desirable for public as well as private purposes that you should be engaged in that office. . . .

Growing up in Virginia

Albemarle County, lying in the shadow of the Blue Ridge Mountains, was still wild and thinly settled country when Willam Lewis went off to the wars in 1776. He left his young wife with their children, Jane and Meriwether, at the family home on Locust Hill by Ivy Creek near Charlottesville. He served as a lieutenant, receiving no pay and providing his own equipment. That was the way Virginians felt about liberty in 1776. When he came home on leave in 1779 he contracted pneumonia and died. Later his widow married John Marks and the family moved to frontier lands in Georgia.

There were now five children in the family, Jane, Meriwether, and Reuben Lewis, and John Marks's two children, Mary and John. They were all growing up together on the edge of the Indian-infested wilderness. One night when they were camping, there was a big scare—an Indian attack. In the wild confusion Meriwether was the only one with enough presence of mind to empty a bucket of water on the campfire so that they could not be seen by an enemy lurking in the forest darkness.

Meriwether loved the woods. When he was eight years old he would go with the hounds on a coon hunt at night with torches. Neighbors said that when a treed coon saw him aim his gun, the coon would holler, "Don't shoot, Meriwether, I'll come down." Then they would slap each other on the back and roar with laughter. It was an old frontier joke that was often told about a good hunter.

Meriwether began to shoot up lean and lanky as a cornstalk. "Time you was learning about something besides coon and possum hunting," said Mother Marks in her determined way. So he went back from the border country to Charlottesville, where his uncle arranged for him to go to the school of that excellent scholar and kindly gentleman, Parson Matthew Maury.

Meriwether took his studies seriously, as he had coon hunting. In the next few years, under one teacher and another, he studied the hodgepodge of subjects that made up the education of a Virginia gentleman of that day. He studied history, Latin, geography, and mathematics, with a little botany and good manners thrown in. His spelling always remained personal and imaginative. He would spell some words three or four different ways, all of them wrong.

School vacations he loved to spend alone in the woods, drinking in the magic and mystery of their ancient peace and beauty. He liked to blaze a westward trail alone in an untrod wilderness.

When he was eighteen and through with schooling, he brought his mother back from Georgia to the old home at Locust

Hill. It was a tradition of Virginia families that a young gentleman should choose as a profession the law, medicine, or the army. His father had been a soldier, so Meriwether decided on the army.

School of Experience

When President Washington called for volunteers to put down the "Whiskey Rebellion," Meriwether volunteered in the Virginia militia as a private and marched to Pittsburgh. The angry distillers of corn whisky dispersed to set up secret stills in the vastnesses of the Alleghenies. The so-called "Whiskey Rebellion" was put down without firing a shot, and the government was safe. Meriwether was then transferred to the regular army. It was a school of action and experience in which he would learn much that he would need to know in the great adventure for which destiny had chosen him.

Soldiers were needed in the wild Northwest territories where Indians were raiding the backwoods settlements and stations, burning and scalping, in a last fierce effort to hold the forest homes of their ancestors. General St. Clair had led a poorly equipped and ill-provisioned expedition against the Indians, which had ended in defeat. After that disaster, President Washington put his old Revolutionary general, Anthony Wayne, in command of the western army to clear the Northwest of the Indians. This was "Mad Anthony" Wayne, who had taken Stony Point with the bayonet on a dark night long ago. Now his first job was to build an efficient fighting force out of the discouraged veterans and shiftless volunteers of St. Clair's army, who still remained at Pittsburgh.

First of all there must be discipline. There was daily drill in all sorts of weather, inspections and practice in the Manual of Arms. The pleasant custom of sleeping on guard duty was discouraged by a prescribed number of lashes on the bare back of the offender. There was no more talking back to superiors by independent privates; no more backslapping or poking of officers' noses by easy-going frontier militiamen. Young Lewis learned how, with axes and plenty of timber, to put up a weatherproof, bulletproof fort in the shortest possible time. He learned how an army can move warily through the wilderness without being surprised from front or rear.

When the army was ready, General Wayne put on a vigorous campaign in the forests of northern Indiana. At the battle of Fallen Timbers he decisively defeated the Indians under the great chief Tecumseh. In this campaign, Lewis renewed an old-time friendship with William Clark of Kentucky, the brother of George Rogers Clark of Vincennes and Kaskaskia fame. Lewis was assigned to the Chosen Rifle Company which Clark commanded.

They were a pair of tall, handsome soldiers, cool and proud fighters, as well as courteous gentlemen, with the gaiety of their exuberant Virginia blood. Both were experts with rifles and horses and gallant and chivalrous with the girls. They could give and take orders and carry out assignments with thoroughness and efficiency. They had the same tastes and background, with enough temperamental differences to make interesting companionship. The red-head Clark was sociable and direct, a frontiersman born and bred. Lewis was of a complex nature, sometimes moody and introspective. Lights and shadows moved behind the deep-set gray eyes that looked out under a long forelock. His long, sharp nose and sensitive mouth reminded some of his friends of the pictures of Napoleon.

Clark soon left the army and returned to Louisville. Lewis remained, to be promoted to captain, serving as paymaster for his regiment. His duties took him up and down the Mississippi and Ohio Rivers and through the Northwest wilderness to outlying army posts. He liked the order and discipline of army life, and travel through the wild country gave variety and adventure to the dullness of army routine.

Coming back to Pittsburgh headquarters in February, 1801, he found a letter awaiting him. His eyes glowed as he read:

> . . . Your knowledge of the Western country, and of the army and of its interests and relations has rendered it desirable for public as well as private purposes that you should be engaged in that office. . . .
>
> If these or any other views which your own reflections may suggest should present the office of my private secretary as worthy of acceptance you will make me happy in accepting it. It has been solicited by several, who will have no answer till I hear from you. Should you accept, it would be necessary that you should wind up whatever affairs you are engaged in as expeditiously as your own and the public interest will admit, and repair to this place. And that immediately on receipt of this you inform me by letter of your determination. It would be necessary that you wait on Gen. Wilkinson and obtain his approbation, and his aid in making such arrangements as may render your absence as little injurious to the service as may be. I wrote him on this subject.
>
> Accept assurances of the esteem of Dear Sir
>
> your friend and servant
> Th: Jefferson

Lewis accepted at once. After winding up his army affairs, he rode off on the long rough road across Pennsylvania to Washington. He wondered if this could really be happening to him, or if it was only a dream, that he was to be the trusted friend of his boyhood hero and secretary to the President of the United States of America.

For ten years and more the President and his young secretary had shared the dream of an expedition of discovery and exploration beyond the Mississippi, across the unknown western wilderness to the Pacific. Now they spent hours together, planning the details that would make it a reality.

From secret sources somewhere in the mysterious Stony Mountains, two great rivers flowed east and west. The Missouri wound eastward like a great snake across the vast plains to the Mississippi. The Columbia rushed down the western slopes to the Pacific Ocean. Perhaps these rivers made an almost continuous water way across the continent. What did all the vast wilderness between contain? No one knew.

Lewis estimated the costs of equipment and supplies, planned the route and timing and the number of men required. The President procured an authorization of the expedition from Congress "for the purpose of extending the external commerce of the United States," and an appropriation of twenty-five hundred dollars. The real purpose was to be kept a secret.

On an expedition so hazardous it was clear that there must be two leaders, so that, in case something should happen to one, the other could carry on. Lewis thought of the young men of action he had known, who were capable and courageous under fire and in difficulties. Who but red-headed Lieutenant William Clark?

With the President's approval Lewis sent off a letter to his friend in Louisville, explaining the expedition and asking Clark to share the command. He wrote:

> If there is anything in this enterprise, which would induce you to participate with me in its fatigues, its dangers and its honors, believe me there is no man on earth with whom I should feel equal pleasure in sharing them as with yourself.

Would William Clark go? Would a duck take to water? Would a young Kentucky thoroughbred race? "My friend, I can assure you that no man lives with whom I would prefer to undertake and share the difficulties of such a trip than yourself. My friend, I join you with hand and heart," wrote back Billy Clark to his old comrade in arms.

The War Department refused to appoint Clark a captain, making him a second lieutenant in the Artillery. But always on the long journey it was "Captain Clark" with Lewis and the men, and the two stood equal in rank and undivided in spirit throughout the great adventure.

Preparation: Washington, D.C., to Pittsburgh, Pa., July 5 to August 31, 1803

Two thousand five hundred dollars was a lot of money in 1803, but Captain Lewis had to make it go a long way in fitting out an expedition of some forty-five men for eighteen months or more. He had to think beforehand of everything that would be needed. When they were two thousand miles up the Missouri it would be too late.

He went to Lancaster, Harpers Ferry, and Philadelphia,

assembling supplies, arms, ammunition, tools, scientific instruments, medicine, and gaudy trinkets for the Indian trade, such as beads, paint, flags, bronze medals with Jefferson's head on one side and hands clasped in peace on the other.

He bought a swivel cannon that could be mounted and fired in any direction; an air gun—a novelty that would be invaluable if ammunition ran out; and a vast quantity of the famous Doctor Rush's Pills, "Good for Whatever Ails You." At the forge at Harpers Ferry an iron boat frame was fashioned; it could be fitted together and covered with birch bark like a canoe. It weighed only a hundred pounds and was named the *Experiment.*

At Philadelphia Lewis studied with scientists the art of determining latitude and longitude and the mysteries of taking "astronomical observations." He would need to use everything he could learn. In the whole expedition there was not a doctor, a scientist, or an artist. The two captains would have to do their best at being each or all of these. Finally he made arrangements for shipment of all supplies to Pittsburgh by wagon.

Lewis spent the winter in the Pittsburgh boat yards supervising the building of the "batteau," or river barge, which would carry the main part of the expedition. The boat builders were addicted to hard liquor and caused exasperating delays. It was August 31 before the barge was launched and started down the Ohio. Near Cincinnati the river was so low that Lewis hired local ox teams to haul the heavy barge over the sandbars. It was October before he reached Louisville, where Clark was impatiently waiting with a number of young Kentuckians, all eager for the trip.

Colts of Democracy: Winter at Wood's River, 1803-1804

By the time the expedition had reached the Mississippi and pushed up to St. Louis it was too late in the season to start up the Missouri. So they set up their winter camp on the American side of the river at the Rivière du Bois, or Woods River, directly opposite the mouth of the Missouri.

Here the men were put to work at drill, rifle practice, hunting, making maple sugar, and building the pirogues. These last were two light flat-bottomed cargo boats propelled by oars and sail.

The men had all been hand-picked by the captains for strength, skill, and intelligence. Seasoned campaigners and Indian fighters laughed at cocky young greenhorns from Virginia. Army men swapped yarns with backwoods hunters and trappers. Strangers sized each other up around the campfires. In the ordeal ahead they were soon to learn the stuff each was made of.

Sergeants Floyd, Ordway, and Pryor were army regulars; Drewyer was a French-Canadian, a lean, silent half-breed who knew the Indian sign language and was a master craftsman of the wilderness. Sixteen-year-old George Shannon, the youngest of all, had run away from home and school, hungry for adventure. The Fields brothers, Reuben and Joseph, were athletic Kentuckians. Pat Gass, with his Irish brogue, was a fine carpenter as well as a professional soldier, and John Colter was a man born to the wilderness. Cruzatte was a one-eyed French riverman whose fiddling was to be the life of the party. There was York, Clark's huge Negro slave, a good cook, an easy laugher and dancer to Cruzatte's fiddling. They were all untamed colts of democracy—high, wide, foxy men—footloose and free and rarin' to go. As a mascot, they had Scannon, Lewis's intelligent Newfoundland dog.

In March news came from Washington that Mr. Jefferson had purchased all of the Louisiana territory from Napoleon for fifteen million dollars. Captain Lewis went to St. Louis to take part in the ceremonies of the formal transfer and saw the flags of Spain and France hauled down and the gay striped flag of the United States run up. He was to carry the flag across American territory all the way to the Pacific.

By May the Missouri was clear of ice. The last bale of goods was stored aboard the little fleet, and on May 14, 1804, the barge and the two pirogues pushed up the Missouri. Clark wrote:

> I set out at 4 o'clock P.M. in the presence of many of the neighboring inhabitants, and proceeded on under a jentle breese up the Missouri.

Twenty miles up the river they stopped at the little French village of St. Charles, where Captain Lewis, arriving from St. Louis, joined the party. On the third day they shifted the cargo from the stern to the bow of the barge to prevent the river snags from ripping through the bottom.

The Barge

"A bas les perches," bawled the one-eyed Cruzatte from the stern deck where he stood at the tiller. The oarsmen facing aft lowered their long poles till they caught on the river bottom. Throwing their weight forward on the poles as one man, they pushed down the cleated catwalks along the gunwales of the boat. When the lead man reached the stern, Cruzatte shouted, "Levez les perches." The men lifted their poles and returned to the bow. The barge had pushed several lengths upstream. This routine was repeated with mechanical regularity hour after hour.

When the channel was too deep for the poles, twenty-two men manned the long oars and pulled the barge steadily against the current. Where it was possible to walk or scramble along the shore, the men towed her by a thousand-foot length of "cordelle" attached to the top of the mast. A guide rope, or bridle, fastened to the ring in the bow kept her from swinging sideways. In the bow a husky lookout or "bosseman" kept her clear of the banks with a long pole. When there was an obstacle on the bank, the cordelle was taken upstream and tied to a tree. The men on the boat then pulled the barge around the obstruction. This was called warping.

The shifting prairie wind was a pusher and booster that often puffed out the barge's big square sail and doubled her speed. Sometimes the wind put on a big show, with thunder and lightning and lashing rain that swooped out of a black cloud, roaring down from the northwest, bending the willows, lashing the water into great waves, and blowing blinding clouds of sand and spray down the river until they had to tie up under a lee shore until the storm was over.

The barge had ten-foot decks fore and aft. The forward cabin was for the captains and the after cabin was used as a sick bay and for the crew. Along the inside of the barge were lockers with doors that could be raised to make a rampart against attacks.

There were two small escort boats, or pirogues. The larger was known as the red pirogue and was manned by seven French voyageurs. The smaller was called the white pirogue, and had a crew of six soldiers. It was planned that the barge was to return from the winter camp on the upper river to St. Louis with specimens and reports for the President in Washington.

At night the men camped and cooked, ate and slept, ashore.

PART II

Up the Missouri

The River

Meriwether Lewis and William Clark
Wrote in their journals after dark
Of all they had seen in the livelong day
Up the Missouri all the way;

Of the surly Sioux in their feathers and pride
Stalking down to the riverside
Out of the plains and the high Black Hills
In their wampum and beads and porcupine quills;

Of beavers and bears and buffalo herds;
Of pelicans, swans, and sweet-singing birds;
Of black bears robbing the honey bees
And chasing the hunters up the trees;

Of white bears charging with foaming jaws
And fiery eyes and terrible claws;
Of plunging ponies with flying manes
And buffalo thundering over the plains.

They drank of the wilderness mystery,
And the wild sweet wine of liberty;
Its splendor and beauty filled their eyes
With sunset pageants in western skies.

Up the Missouri

THE TWO tall captains in their army uniforms stood on the forward deck in the light rain. A gentle breeze filled the sail and the rhythmic strokes of the twenty-two oarsmen drove the barge steadily upstream against the stiff current. At last they were through with the farewell dinners and balls, the toasts and speeches, the cheering and bowing. Before them lay the shining path of the winding river calling to adventure. The Missouri was calling them across the mysterious prairies to the unknown mountains. Each day unfolded a new wild world in which the unexpected waited around each bend of the twisting river.

At the bow, Cruzatte the riverman with his one eye scoured the changing face of the waters, reading in the swirls and eddies the signs of snags, "sawyers," and sandbars lying in ambush just beneath the surface. The corps was divided into three "messes," commanded by Sergeants Ordway, Floyd, and Pryor. Drewyer and Colter hunted along the shores, bringing in bear, deer, beaver, and other game for the pot. Out of the river, the men yanked fat catfish. They camped at night on the low shores of willow-covered islands. The weary voyagers sniffed hungrily the fragrance of campfire supper at the end of each day's pull.

The captains took turns daily at walking along the shore. Clark would take Drewyer, Colter, Shannon, and York for company. Lewis liked to go alone through the wooded bottomlands or across the empty plains. After supper the captains sat on their bunks in the forecastle and wrote out the day's record, which they kept at the President's express order. Both were keen reporters, but it is hard to say which was the worst speller. Lewis used the most words, recording what he thought, along with what he saw. Clark put down facts briefly. Together, day by day, they kept a detailed and vivid record of all they saw and did.

After supper as the men sat gazing into the fire, Cruzatte would draw his fiddle from a leather bag and strike up a lively dance tune. In a moment hands were clapping and heels stomping in the antic capers of booted dancers. Suddenly York would leap into the center of the circle and dance down all comers with a grotesque buck and wing.

Through the night there were always two sentinels on guard. The mournful wolf-howls rose to the burning stars across the blackness of moving waters. As the men turned out in the gray dawn they sometimes shook a live rattlesnake from a blanket or pillow, where he had crept just to be warm and friendly. That helped to liven one up for the day's work.

The captains gave names to the rivers that poured prairie soil and sand into the Missouri and to the numberless long willow islands dreaming in its rolling torrent. On the Fourth of July they fired off the cannon with cheers and named the creek they were passing "Independence." They exchanged news with traders coming down from the Indian country on rafts. One of these was a Mr. Dorion who had lived among the Sioux for twenty years. He was engaged to return upriver as interpreter.

The men were learning that each depended on the others and the lives of all might hang on the action of a single one. They were in country where, if a man slept on guard duty, stole whisky, or disobeyed orders, it might have dangerous consequences for the whole party. Offenders were tried by court-martial conducted by the sergeants, with the men as jury. So many lashes on the bare back, according to the crime, was the army punishment meted out to the guilty. Two deserters slipped off into the prairie. Drewyer, keen as a blood hound, trailed them to the Indian village where they were hiding. One—the Frenchman who was called "La Liberty"—escaped, but Drewyer brought back Moses Ross, the other deserter. He was tried by court-martial and found guilty. He was sentenced to run the gantlet four times. He was then dismissed from the corps. He was to go back with the French voyageurs.

The spirit of the corps was shaping its unruly members into a disciplined and unbeatable team. They grew tough-skinned and steel-muscled in their daily tussle with the river current, and brown as Indians under the blistering summer sun. They drank muddy river water and broke out with painful boils. The captains had to act as amateur doctors and treated every ailment from sunstroke to snakebite with equal ignorance—and with equal success.

They passed through the Osage Indian country without seeing an Indian. It was the hunting season and the tribes were out on the prairie following the buffalo. Along the river banks were the melancholy sites of old Indian villages that had been abandoned because of war or smallpox. Along the river bottoms, wild grapes, plums, and berries were ripening in abundance.

The President's instructions read, "In all your intercourse with the natives, treat them in the most friendly and conciliatory manner which their own conduct will admit." A good many in the corps had dealt with the Indians over the sights of their rifles. Peacemaking might be a difficult and delicate business. The various nations along the river had individual peculiarities and temperamental differences and each would have to be dealt with accordingly. Jefferson had added, "To your own discretion therefore must be left the degree of danger you may risk, and the point at which you should decline, only saying we wish you to err on the side of your safety, and bring back your party safe, even if it be with less information."

In two months they had toiled six hundred miles up the winding river. The expedition had now come to the mouth of the river Platte, which flowed from the Rockies across a thousand miles of prairie to the Missouri. Old-timers later were to refer to the Platte as a river "one thousand miles long and an inch deep."

Indians at Last: Council Bluffs

Drewyer, hunting along shore, had surprised three Indians ting up an elk in the high prairie grass. They were friendly a were sent back with an invitation to their tribe to meet with th white men on the river.

Lewis, scanning the prairie with his spyglass, was the first to see the moving shapes in the long grass, coming over the prairie.

He could count fourteen horsemen riding at top speed, their copper skins glistening in the sunlight and their long hair streaming in the wind. They dashed up and pulled in their lathering horses. A Frenchman, who was with them, came forward. He said that the party were Otoes and Missouri from a nearby camp, and that they would sit in council with the white men tomorrow. The captains gave them a hearty supper, after which the Indians rolled up in their blankets for the night.

Next morning the Otoes came and sat in the shade of the boat sail, which was spread for the occasion. The flag was run up and the corps paraded and saluted the colors. The swivel gun was fired with a terrific bang. The Indians looked on with expressionless faces. After the peace pipe had been passed Lewis arose and made a speech, which the Frenchman translated. The captain explained that the Great White Father had taken over the land from the French and Spanish, who would come no more. The White Father wished his red children to be at peace. When there was peace on the river, the American traders would come, bringing guns and all the good things the Indians wanted.

Each of the chiefs made a long speech in reply, saying they were full of joy at the change of government and would welcome the American traders; and they asked the white chiefs to make peace for them with their dreaded enemies the Mahas.

After the speeches the captains presented the chiefs with medals, powder, whisky, paint, and bright cloth. The fierce faces glowed with delight. Gay with the new geegaws and the whisky, they rode off over the prairie. The first encounter with the Indians was definitely a success. They called the low hills where they had met "Council Bluffs." This was to be a good site for a trading post, a fort, and a town in the days to come.

The little fleet toiled on up the snag-infested river that now wound and looped like a snake. They stopped to climb a cliff of yellow sandstone three hundred feet high to see the burial mound of Black Bird, the renowned Indian chief. He had been famous for his magic powers and could even foretell when his enemies would die. The effect of his terrible "medicine" was due to the use of arsenic, which he had obtained from the white men. He himself had died of the smallpox and had been buried seated on his horse where he could forever look down the river. The Indians still left food there to comfort his departed spirit. The white men placed a flag on the pole that marked his grave and continued on up the river.

Drewyer set fire to the prairie as a signal to the Indians that the white men had come to trade. In the tall prairie grass they came upon the charred ruins of a Maha village. It had been burned after the smallpox had wiped out four hundred families. Farther on the men seined in a creek and made a huge catch of hundreds of fish. It was a welcome change of diet.

Sergeant Floyd was taken suddenly and violently ill. Captain Clark tended the sick man with all the care and science he knew. Next day Floyd said, "I am going to leave you. I want you to write me a letter."

Clark wrote down his last words. Gallant Charles Floyd crossed the last frontier into the undiscovered country. He was buried on the top of the bluff with the honors due a brave soldier; and the place of his interment marked by a cedar post on which the name and the day of his death were inscribed. He was the only man of the party to die on the trip. Patrick Gass, the stocky Irish carpenter, was appointed by the captains to take Floyd's place as mess sergeant.

Treating with the Sioux

A party left the river and trekked across the prairie in the August heat to see the "Mountain of the Little People." The Indians believed this flat-topped mound was inhabited by evil spirits who shot deadly arrows at all who came near. The white men found no traces of the Little People. As they returned to the river they picked and ate delicious grapes, wild plums, and ripe berries.

That night they again set fire to the prairie to signal to the Indians that they had come to trade. Two days later an Indian swam out to the boat with the news that a Sioux encampment was near by. Next day they camped at Calumet Bluff to await the Indians. Sergeant Pryor and a party had been sent twelve miles over the prairie to the camp with an invitation. The Indians came out and wanted to carry the white chief on a buffalo robe. Pryor explained that he was only a messenger sent by the white chiefs to invite them to their camp on the river. The Indians gave the white messengers a feast of stewed dog. The hungry men liked it. It was their first taste of man's best friend.

Five Sioux chiefs and about seventy men and boys came with Pryor to the camp. The next day the Sioux sat in a circle under an oak tree by the river, as Captain Lewis made his speech about peace and the advantages of trading with the Americans. Paint and ribbons, uniforms and medals, were given to the chiefs, and the pipe of peace went around the beaming circle.

The Sioux chiefs now retired for a private council, while the lean young braves shot magnificently with the bows and arrows for prizes of tobacco and trinkets which the captains distributed to the winners. That night there was a dog feast and dancing around the campfires to the Indian drums.

Next morning the two captains in their uniforms took their place at the Indian council. The five chiefs in their white buffalo robes sat in a row smoking the peace pipe. Feathers decorated the black braids of long hair which fell over their shoulders. Their white buffalo robes were painted with crude pictures of battle scenes. Bear-claw necklaces gleamed at their throats. The eldest chief rose and spoke:

> I see before me my great father's two sons. You see me, and the rest of our chiefs and warriors. We are very poor; we have neither powder nor ball, nor knives; and our women and children at the village have no clothes. I wish that as my brothers have given me a flag and a medal, they would give something to those poor people, or let them stop and trade with the first boats that come up the river. I will make peace with the Pawnees and Mahas together, and make peace between them; but it is better that I should do it than my great father's sons, for they will listen to me more readily. I will also take some chiefs to your country in the spring; but before that I cannot leave home.

The long speech continued with pauses as Dorion translated. At the end the younger chiefs arose and spoke in the order of their rank. They repeated the request and said they would open their ears to the white brothers' advice. The captains asked many questions and filled their notebooks with Indian lore. In the tribe were four warriors who were the sole survivors of a society which was sworn never to retreat in the face of danger. Once when marching single file across a frozen river, they had come to a hole in the ice. The leader kept straight on and disappeared forever. The rest were saved only by being dragged off by their friends. These braves were honored even above the chiefs.

Dorion was ordered to remain with the Sioux. He was instructed to make peace among the warring tribes and to persuade some of the chiefs to accompany him on a visit to the President in Washington. Peacemaking was a difficult assignment along the upper Missouri in 1804.

For two weeks the corps had been deeply anxious about young Shannon. Their two horses had strayed and Shannon had been sent ashore to bring them in. When he had not returned after several days, Drewyer and Colter had vainly scoured the shores for traces of him. Sixteen days later, coming around a bend in the river, they sighted a lean horseman riding down the riverbank. It was Shannon. He had found the horses, but thought the party had got ahead of him, so he had pushed on for fifteen days. Nearly starved, he had finally given up and turned back just in time to meet them. Many times the men were sent out alone on dangerous missions, and always they returned in safety.

The river was still a mile wide, but definitely shallower with more and meaner sandbars. Beyond the river bluffs, the prairie was alive with vast herds of buffalo and elk and the swift and beautiful antelope. The river teemed with beaver, swans, geese, duck, and sometimes pelicans. A sandbar on which they were camped suddenly washed out from under them. They barely got the boats out from under the bank before it too caved in. The river was a tricky antagonist.

One evening three Indian boys swam out to the boats with word that two Sioux encampments were on the river just above them. They were sent back with presents of tobacco to the chiefs and an invitation to a council at the riverside.

There was great excitement in the Sioux camps over the news that the white men in their great winged canoe were coming up the river. Black Buffalo, the ranking chief, wished to trade with the white men. There would be presents and he was first in the receiving line. But the Partisan, also a powerful chief, wanted to

stop the expedition. If his braves could carry out a surprise attack, there would be much loot and many scalps. The younger warriors were eager to follow him. But the ever-watchful enemy always kept their floating fortress in the middle of the river, safe from surprise attacks.

Sixty braves, magnificent in savage finery, came down to the council with the captains. Black Buffalo wore a white buffalo robe decorated with porcupine quills and a headdress of eagle feathers. The Partisan was painted from head to foot in patterns of yellow and red and green. His leggings were trimmed with the scalps of his enemies and two fine skunk skins dragged from the heels of his beaded moccasins. He was a fierce and splendid image of terror out of a nightmare.

The captains were impressive in their uniforms with cocked hats and swords, though the soldiers were shabby in their worn deerskin shirts and leggings. But the bright flag in the wind and the perfect precision of their drill made a gallant show. Without Dorion, the interpreter, they could not understand each other's speeches, although the presents were accepted by the Indian chiefs with the usual pleasure and excitement. In the visiting back and forth from boat to shore, the Indians had been surly and insolent and a quarrel between Clark and the Partisan nearly came to blows, but Black Buffalo had intervened and kept the peace. The two chiefs had then come aboard for the night. Altogether it had been a tense and trying day. They called their camp that night "Bad-humoured Island."

Next day both sides were more friendly. The Sioux were preparing to celebrate a recent victory over their enemies, the Mahas, with a delicious dog feast and a ceremonial scalp dance. The shores were lined with excited squaws and children eager to see the white strangers. The captains went ashore and were carried triumphantly into the Indian camp on white buffalo robes. In the evening, they sat in the council circle with seventy solemn Indian warriors. Black Buffalo rose and pointed the ceremonial pipe to the heavens, to the earth, and to the four points of the

compass. He was addressing the Great Spirit, the Father of the Universe. The white men watched with awe the solemn rituals of the stone age. The pipe went around the circle. Black Buffalo made a long speech which the white men could not understand. The stewed dog was served from the kettles with horn spoons. The captains tasted it sparingly and looked hungrily at the great pile of jerked buffalo meat which the tribe had presented them. Wood was heaped on the fires and the center of the circle cleared for the dance.

Suddenly the drums rolled and the rattles sounded. The young braves began a chant, accented with shrill yells. On each side of the fire the squaws swayed and shuffled forward and back in two lines, carrying long poles from which hung fresh scalps. The rhythm of the drumbeat and the chanting bound the tribe together in a mystic union with their ancient gods of earth and wind and sky and filled their hearts with strength and joy. In the intervals a storyteller raised his voice and recited a tale out of the immemorial storehouse of tribal lore. A new dance began. The warriors stamped around the fire, bending to the earth and leaping up, and uttering high-pitched yells as they brandished their war clubs. Hour after hour, in the flickering light, fantastic figures were vignetted against the blue darkness in a weird pantomime. At last the weary white men politely excused themselves and went back to the boat.

Next day there was more friendly visiting. The squaws and braves marveled at the air gun and the swivel cannon, which were fired off for their benefit. The captains visited the skin teepees of the Sioux. These portable houses of the plains could be taken down in a few minutes and packed on the pole travoirs that were dragged by ponies. Each tent housed ten or fifteen people. They were cool in summer and warm in winter. Huddled behind the camp, the captains found a miserable group of some twenty-five women and children. They were captives taken in the recent raid on the Mahas. The Sioux had taken seventy-five scalps and destroyed forty teepees. The captains gave the dejected prisoners awls and needles, and asked the Sioux chiefs to show them mercy.

Their Great Father wished his red children to make peace with their enemies and spare the prisoners. A grateful captive warned Drewyer that the Sioux were plotting to stop the boats.

That night the watch was doubled and the guns primed. The rest of the party went ashore to another feast and dance. As they returned after midnight, the pirogue struck against the cable of the barge and broke it. All hands turned out to right the barge as she started to drift downstream. The Indians spread the alarm to their camp that the Mahas were attacking. Sixty of the warriors watched on shore all night. The captains thought that they were watching to see that the white men did not go on up the river.

Dragging for the lost anchor in the morning, the men could not recover it. They finally put the reluctant Indians ashore and cast off.

The Sioux followed along the banks, signaling and beckoning. Farther on another band appeared and signaled for a council. The captains called back and told them to go down the river and they would find out from Mr. Dorion all they wanted to know. Black Buffalo was still aboard. Singly, and in groups, the Sioux continued to hail them as the barge advanced up the river, but the boats passed by without stopping.

There were more sandbars and a high cold wind blew from the northwest. The barge struck a hidden snag and keeled over dangerously. Black Buffalo was so frightened that he dived ignominiously under a bunk. When things quieted down, he asked to be put ashore. He said that, as his white friends were now safely through the Sioux country, he wished to go home. He was put ashore with presents of a knife, an army blanket, and a twist of tobacco. Black Buffalo, friend of the white man, waved a solemn farewell as the boat disappeared up the winding river.

At Fort Mandan: October 27, 1804, to April 7, 1805

The captains looked at each other and sighed with relief. They were mighty glad to be safe, out of the Sioux country. They had remained calm and cool when bows were bent and itching trigger fingers might have caused sudden tragedy. This took a more difficult kind of courage than actual fighting. By the President's express orders they were to keep peace with and among the Indians. Besides, bucking the Missouri was difficult enough without carrying on a war at the same time. So, at each new encounter along the river, the captains advised, questioned, cajoled, explained, bartered, bribed, and amused, but seldom threatened the touchy chiefs.

They stopped and visited the three Ricara villages perched high on the banks above the river. The Ricara were a fine-looking, friendly people. They agreed to the white men's peace proposals and amazed them by refusing to drink their whisky. The wise Ricara said they were surprised "that their father [the President] should present to them that which would make them fools."

It was getting cold and the men shivered in the chill October mornings, wondering at the indifference of the naked Indian chiefs to the cold. They were now coming to the country of the Mandans and along the shores they passed the ruins of old Mandan villages that had been abandoned because of the fierce attacks of the Sioux. In the debris were skulls of men and animals, telling of old tragedies.

Soon live Mandans were crowding the shores and bluffs to see the marvelous strangers. When the boats stopped below the first village, crowds of curious braves, squaws, and children came aboard to see the wonders. The great chief of all the Mandans, the Black Cat, came to meet the captains and agreed to call the chiefs of the five villages to a council to hear the white men tell why they had come to their country. Next day the chiefs assembled and the sail was put up as a screen from the high wind. The men paraded, the flag was run up, and off went the swivel gun. Captain Lewis made his speech. In the middle of it, the oldest Indian chief grew restless and interrupted rudely to say he must go, because he had remembered that his village might be attacked by the Shoshones. Another chief sharply rebuked him for his bad manners. The old fellow sat down meekly and remained silent until the conclusion of the speech. Flags, medals, and bright coats were presented to the chiefs according to rank, and as a grand climax the corn mill, which the party no longer needed, was presented to the Mandan nation as a whole. The Indians preferred their own way of grinding corn and broke up the mill to use its iron for arrowheads.

VISITING THE BLACK CAT

Captain Clark, Drewyer, the interpreter, Colter, and York landed from the pirogue and walked up the shore toward the Mandan village to visit the Black Cat, the great chief of the Mandans. They could see the rounded tops of the lodges on the high bluffs silhouetted sharply against the sky. Smoke rose from the holes in their roofs. They could see Indians standing on the rooftops scanning the river. On the beach under the cliffs, a fleet of bull boats rested bottoms up. The bend of the river protected two sides of the town by water, and on the land side a log palisade had been built of posts, spaced for firing between them. Inside the palisade was a trench which further guarded the defenders from their enemies. This site afforded the best possible protection.

As the visitors walked through the bottomland toward the village, they passed gardens of Indian corn, melons, and beans tended by squaws. At the entrance to the palisade, they were welcomed by the whole village. The excited Indians led Clark to the chief's lodge.

York wandered around the village to be admired by the Indian girls. He flexed his muscles, growled and showed his teeth, horribly frightening the Indian children. He said he was a wild animal that had been captured and tamed by Captain Clark. Several times he danced, clapping his hands in rhythm. The squaws screamed with delight.

Captain Clark was ushered into the chief's lodge and seated near the fire beside his host on a white buffalo robe. The smoke hole in the roof let in a column of light. A buffalo robe was thrown about his shoulders and he was handed the lighted peace pipe.

As his eyes became accustomed to the semi-darkness, Clark could see the shields and weapons hanging from the roof posts. The dirt floor was some ninety feet across and packed almost glass smooth. Behind the screens of buffalo hide, he could see the wooden bed-frames, on which were stretched buffalo hides.

Dogs, pups, and numerous children rolled together on the floor. Through the smoky haze, he could see the chief's wives visiting with relatives and guests. The horses were brought in, stabled for the night, and fed the juicy bark of cottonwood trees. There was a pungent smell of woodsmoke, stable, cooking meat, and Indian.

Black Cat wanted the captain to know that he approved the idea of a general peace. The women could then work in the fields and take off their moccasins to sleep at night without fear of attack. He told them that there had been great hope among the village of everyone getting plenty of presents and all but the chiefs had been considerably disappointed. Black Cat himself would accept Clark's invitation to visit the President later on. He gave Clark twelve bushels of corn and returned some goods stolen from white traders by irresponsible persons. Clark made a friendly reply in his most impressive manner, and presented the chief with a red coat with gold braid. When he left he felt sure that his party could spend a peaceful winter with the friendly Mandans as neighbors.

That evening the dry prairie grass accidentally took fire. In a few minutes, the flames were raging furiously across the plain. Several Indians were burned badly and two fatally before it had passed. A squaw who found she could not carry her boy to safety threw a fresh buffalo hide over him. Later he was pulled out from under the hide, alive and unharmed. The Indians said it was a miracle of the Great Spirit, because the boy was half white. The white men said it was, of course, the damp buffalo skin. The white men explained how things happened. The Indians accounted for *why* things happened.

That evening, Indian visitors came to the boat, asking the white men to dance for them. Cruzatte struck up the fiddle and the boys put on a rollicking program with York as the star performer. Everybody went to bed in a very good humor.

Winter Quarters at Fort Mandan, November 8, 1904

At night the men shivered under their blankets and the ground froze hard. The glittering northern lights shot their changing phantom shapes into the sky and danced their weird ghost ballet. Ice began to float down the river. It was time to find winter quarters. Clark selected a site on a wooded point under the bluffs, a mile below the village, and laid out a triangular fort.

The men set to work with axes and saws among the cottonwood trees. They built two rows of log cabins set at right angles. There were four cabins in a row, each fourteen feet square. Each had a stone fireplace and a puncheon floor and ceiling, and the walls were chinked with mud. On the third side was built a long curving palisade of stout logs. By November 20, the fort was finished. At night, in the warm cabins, the tired men turned in under their buffalo robes and snored like lions. It was the first time in six months that they had slept under a roof.

The blizzards came howling down from the Arctic Circle and piled the snowdrifts high against the log walls of Fort Mandan. The temperature dropped to forty-five degrees below zero. The naked Indians played hockey on the frozen river.

Inside the fort everyone was busy. In the blacksmith shop, the Fields brothers shaped little squares of iron into hatchets or "eye-daggs" and traded them for the corn which the Indian women brought in on their strong backs. Shields became famous among the Indians as a restorer of their damaged rifles and ancient muskets, and did a thriving business in barter. Captain Clark was engrossed in a map he was making of the surrounding country. Lewis went with the hunting parties across the snow-covered prairies after the buffalo. The men butchered the buffalo and smoked the meat, or made pemmican. They dressed deerskins and made shirts, moccasins, and leggings. The Indians came and went, but at night the gates were closed and always there was a sentinel on duty. Two little squaws came in one day, as curious as deer. They were Shoshones, who had been captured by the Minnetarees as children. They had been bought as slaves by a French trader named Charbonneau and were now his wives. Charbonneau was hired as an interpreter, and he and his family came to live in the fort. One of the squaws, Sacajawea, was little more than a child. Her black eyes sparkled with intelligence. She was neat, quick, and silent. Until she came to Fort Mandan, she had been an anonymous chattel. In the fort, she was quiet and useful in many ways. Next to Lewis and Clark, she was to become the most famous and best-remembered person in the party. Here, in February, her first baby was born. She called him Jean Baptiste. As the captains came to notice the little squaw, they realized that she would make a valuable guide and interpreter in the Shoshone country, through which they would pass in the spring and where they hoped to secure horses to take them over the mountain passes to the Columbia River.

On Christmas day, the captains were awakened by a discharge of three platoons by the party. The American flag then was hoisted for the first time over the fort. There was skylarking and dancing to Cruzatte's fiddle, as Sacajawea looked on with unblinking eyes. For dinner, "the best provisions we had" were brought out and York cooked some Virginia specialties which were eaten with toasts and cheers. Around the cabin hearths there was song and laughter and the Christmas spirit glowed brightly in the little fort in the frozen heart of the wilderness.

There was more fun on New Year's Day, which began with two shots from the swivel gun and a round of small arms. It was a mild day and a gay party went calling on the Mandan village. They came whooping and dancing among the delighted Indians. York unlimbered a dance and one of the Frenchmen created a sensation by dancing on his hands. The tribe, which was always ready for a frolic, put on a dance in return. Hostilities and suspicions vanished in the good will and gaiety, as white and red men laughed and danced together, on a wilderness New Year's Day.

By the fireside in their warm cabins, the captains received the visiting Indian chiefs and gave them good advice about making and keeping peace. They thawed out frozen Indians and treated them for frostbite, listened to the daily reports of the sergeants, and faithfully wrote down each day's doing in their journals.

SACAGAWEA

Hunger

Providing daily for forty husky feeders in the white wilderness was a heavy responsibility. The elk, deer, and buffalo herds were disappearing and the animals they could shoot were too lean to eat. In the vast bleakness of the snow-covered plain, the starved game was hard to find. The red men endured starvation as a matter of course, like hibernating animals, but most of the white men suffered if they went without food for a single day. The captains did not mean to see the men go hungry if they could help it.

Clark and eighteen hunters started down the frozen river on a hunting expedition. It was a good highway, swept clean of snow in places. They traveled forty miles in two days, killing only two starved buffalo and a lean deer. Next day, they fanned out on the prairie. On the southern slopes of low hills were deer and elk.

They killed forty deer and sixteen elk. The horses were loaded with meat and sent back up the river to the hungry men at the fort. What was left, they boned and stored in a log pen, to keep off the wolves and crows. Next day, they followed the river through another twenty miles of empty wilderness. Then they turned back and three days later reached the fort.

Sleds with four men and three horses went down river to bring in the cached meat. On the way back, they were ambushed and robbed by a party of one hundred Sioux. Next morning, Lewis, with twenty-six men, started off in pursuit. Riding through the Mandan village, he invited the Indians to join the party. Most of the braves were out hunting but a few warriors took up their bows and hatchets and went along. For two days they followed the trail across the dazzling snow of the empty prairie, but to no avail. Coming back along the river bottoms, they found herds of deer and elk. The hunters made a big kill, bagging thirty-six deer and fourteen elk. They brought in three thousand pounds of meat on sleds to the fort. Fort Mandan had met and mastered the hunger and cold of the grim northern winter.

Toward the Unknown

Missouri Dancers

When the river mirrored the yellow moon,
Old Cruzatte struck up a fiddle tune;
Black York laughed and rolled his eye;
He cracked his heels and he leaped high;
He jumped so nimble and frisked so free
He danced off chains for liberty;
He danced out sorrow and he danced out sin;
He danced out bondage and freedom in.
The wolves they howled and the buffalo pranced,
When Cruzatte fiddled and Black York danced.

Red laughter shook the Indian squaws
Till their eyes bugged out and they cracked their jaws;
The chiefs all chuckled and the red braves grinned
And Sergeant Gass hollered, "I'll be skinned!"
The grizzlies waltzed and wiggled their ears,
And the little coyotes gave three cheers;
The beavers jigged till they lost their pants,
When Cruzatte fiddled and Black York danced.

Toward the Unkown

Our vessels consisted of six small canoes, and two large perogues. This little fleet altho' not quite so rispectable as those of Columbus or Capt. Cook, were still viewed by us with as much pleasure as those deservedly famed adventurers ever beheld theirs; and I dare say with quite as much anxiety for their safety and preservation. We were now about to penetrate a country at least two thousand miles in width, on which the foot of civilized man had never trodden; the good or evil it had in store for us was for experiment yet to determine, and these little vessels contained every article by which we were to expect to subsist or defend ourselves. However, as the state of mind in which we are, generally gives the colouring to events, when the imagination is suffered to wander into futurity, the picture which now presented itself to me was a most pleasing one. Enterta[in]ing as I do, the most confident hope of suceeding in a voyage which had formed a da[r]ling project of mine for the last ten years, I could but esteem this moment of my departure as among the most happy of my life. The party are in excellent health and sperits, zealously attached to the enterprise, and anxious to proceed; not a whisper of murmur or discontent to be heard among them, but all act in unison, and with the most perfict harmony.

(Lewis's entry in his journal, April 7, 1805)

Mandan Spring: From Fort Mandan to the Mouth of the Yellowstone, April 7 to 26, 1805

The sun was getting stronger. The ice was breaking up along the shore and frost was coming out of the ground. Lewis wrote in the journal, "the weather exceedingly pleasant," and the men in "high spirits." For weeks the men had been trying to pry the boats out of the ice. Now they were able to haul them up on the banks for repairs. French traders from downriver brought good news. The Ricara were making an alliance with the Mandans and Minnetarees against the Sioux. The Indians were burning off the old dead grass on the prairie, so that their horses and the buffalo could get at the new green that was soon coming. Men went out through the bottomlands selecting trees that could be hollowed into canoes for the upriver journey.

Le Borgne, the great chief of the Minnetarees, came down to visit the fort. He was a huge one-eyed savage, known for his brutality. He had not, before this, come to see the white chiefs. When he arrived, the whole fort turned out to see him and fired off two shots of the cannon in his honor. He announced that if any presents had been sent him, he had never received them. At this hint, he was presented with a medal, flag, and some gaudy ornaments. He was shown the swivel gun, air gun, and other marvels, but he still had something on his mind. He had heard, he said—what was probably but foolish talk—that the visitors had with them a man who was entirely black; if it were so he wanted to see him. York appeared in ebony splendor. The chief walked around him, examining him closely. He tried to wipe off the paint from York's shiny back. He was still doubtful, until York took off his bandana and showed his kinky hair. Le Borgne was amazed, delighted, and convinced.

By mid-March, the ice began to break up and the river to come to life. On the sandbars, the floating ice piled up with a great churning roar. Then the weight of the waters behind the "gorge," or ice jam, would force a passage and carry the whole mass roaring and swirling downstream. The Indians dashed out on the ice and killed buffalo that had been caught on floating cakes of ice while trying to cross the river.

Charbonneau had become very self-important and insisted that he should not be subject to orders like the regular soldiers. The captains were firm and stated they could get along very well without him. He went off in a huff, but as no further attention was paid to him, he returned apologetically and was accepted back into service on the same terms as the soldiers.

The carpenters were hollowing out the cottonwood logs into canoes. These were now light enough to haul to the river to be caulked, where cracks were opening in the wood. The first spring rain came and great flocks of geese and swans patterned the skies. The barge was loaded for the return voyage with specimens for the President—boxes of Indian paraphernalia, animal skins, and skeletons. There were boxes of stuffed birds, snakes, and insects. There were cages containing a burrowing squirrel, a prairie hen, and four magpies, all very much alive. It would be an exciting day at the President's house when they arrived. Lewis sent a long letter to his mother and the joint report on the expedition to Mr. Jefferson. The soldiers scrawled fond messages to their families and friends, sixteen-hundred miles back in the States.

The two pirogues and six canoes were loaded for the upriver journey. Dog Scannon was in and out everywhere, barking and wagging his tail with excitement. Sacajawea's expressionless face hid her wild delight. She was going on with the white men to find her own people. Little Baptiste, strapped to a board on her back, merely blinked and drooled at the strange new world seen from his mother's shoulder. It was early Monday morning, April 6, when they waved farewell to the old barge as she dropped down the river on her sixteen-hundred-mile voyage to St. Louis.

The men took their place in the pirogues and canoes. One after another the little fleet pushed out against the current in the teeth of a strong west wind. They were headed toward the unknown west to find the sources of the Missouri, to cross the shining mountains, and to follow the Columbia down to the Great South Sea.

The Lost World: April 26, 1805

The monstrous buffalo filed down out of the carved hills, and the shaggy bulls sloshed their dripping beards in the river shallows. Along the bottomlands, great herds of elk tore off mouthfuls of the new leaves, and shook their sprouting antlers. The young fawns lifted their ears curiously and gazed with their great tender eyes at the approach of the hunters. The dainty pronghorned antelope flew with incredible bounds over the long slopes of the rolling prairie, and the wolves slunk in the underbrush, watching

to spring and pull down a straying buffalo calf. The ambling white bear reached into the hollow beetree and licked the dripping honey from his paw, while the bee clan swarmed furiously around his great tawny head. So fearless were the gentle prairie grazers that they would hardly move out of the path of the invaders, who sometimes had to drive them off with sticks.

The wind and water of countless seasons had carved the vast land into fantastic shapes and grotesque forms. Sculptured pinnacles towered above the river, like colored dream castles of awe and wonder. The red light of sunset blazed on cliffs and walls that were streaked with bands of orange, green, and scarlet earth. The party explored up the winding Yellowstone, where it wandered into the Missouri, through a treeless land that stretched out endlessly. Buried under the barren hills lay the bones of gigantic lizards who had danced under the moon millions of years before little apelike men crept out of their smoky caves to harass the woolly mastodon. Hidden in the rocks ran rich veins of silver, copper, iron, zinc, lead, and coal. Under their feet, in the sands of the river, lay millions of golden nuggets.

Mostly about Bears: Montana, May 14, 1805

Drewyer found eleven-inch footprints in the wet sand by the river. He was the undisputed king of the mountains and prairie. Every living thing that met him on the trail gave him wide and undisputed room. It was tribute to King Grizzly—the "white bear," as the Indians called him on account of his tawny-colored fur. When he stood on his hind legs, he towered eight to ten feet. On the end of each front paw were five long claws that ripped like knives when driven by a blow of his terrible arm.

Drewyer, Colter, and the Fields brothers had come upon him as he was looking for a beetree in the timber and brush along the river. At the moment he was lying in an open space and when he rose on his hind legs to inspect the strangers, two of the hunters fired into his massive bulk. With a guttural roar the monster charged. The two hunters did not just run—they flew for their lives toward the river and shoved off in the canoe. The other two, who had held their fire, now shot into the bear. He turned and charged after them as they made for the willows. Here they managed to hide, reload, and put several more bullets into him, but the great beast seemed indestructible. He charged after Reuben Fields and pressed so close that Fields jumped from a twenty-foot bank into the river, with the great brute hurtling through the air behind him. He was swimming for the canoe, with the bear just a few feet behind him, when his brother fired from the cliff and drilled a bullet directly through the bear's head. Still green and shaky with fright, the hunters dragged the huge carcass to the shore and stripped off the heavy pelt. Seven shots had passed through the vitals.

Later Captain Lewis barely escaped a pursuing grizzly by jumping into the Missouri. Taking to the river or the nearest tree became standard practice when you ran into a "white bear."

Once, one of the party stumbled on a grizzly concealed in the underbrush. His frightened horse had reared violently, thrown his rider, and dashed off. The man snatched up his rifle and cracked the bear over his sensitive nose. As the dazed monster rubbed this painful member with his paws, the hunter lit out for the nearest tree. White bears cannot climb trees, so Grizzly took up his post underneath to wait for the fruit to fall. All day long the hunter sat in the tree and reflected on a misspent life. At

sundown the bear, possibly remembering that his wife expected him home for supper, ambled off. After a safe interval, the man came down, recovered his horse, and rode safely back to camp.

Through the night these monsters slunk about the camp hoping to raid the larder, but the faithful dog Scannon, growling and bristling, kept them from venturing within the radius of the firelight. Although the men often had to jump, run, or climb for life, no one was ever actually caught by a bear.

An Upset

The same day that the men met their first grizzly, a sudden squall hit the pirogue like a blow and laid the sail flat on the water, where she filled within an inch of her gunwales. Three of the men in the capsizing boat could not swim, and Sacajawea was there with her baby. In the boat were the instruments, papers, medicine, all that was vital to the expedition. As Cruzatte cut the sail loose, she slowly righted. Charbonneau had dropped the rudder and was calling on the saints. Sacajawea in the stern was quickly and coolly gathering in any valuable that was floating. The men were bailing frantically. On the distant shore, Lewis and Clark fired their guns and shouted orders, but nobody heard. "Grab that rudder or I'll shoot you," howled Cruzatte, furiously pointing his gun at Charbonneau.

The men now manned the oars and brought the boat safely to shore. Lewis remembered the adventure "with the utmost trepidation and horror." A bear hunt and a near-shipwreck, on May 14, marked the first anniversary of the start of the expedition.

THE MOUTH OF THE MARIA'S RIVER: JUNE 2, 1805

The river water was clearer now, and through the dry, clear air they caught distant glimpses of snow-capped mountains. The creeks and rivers teemed with the industrious beaver and on the highlands they could see herds of bighorn.

Suddenly, one night, the camp was roused by Scannon's barking and a terrific rushing about in the darkness. A buffalo bull had swum the river and blundered into one of the canoes. Mad with fright, he was charging about the camp among the sleeping men, barely missing trampling on their heads. Finally the bull rushed off into the darkness with Scannon snapping at his heels.

At the foot of a high cliff the men saw and smelled the rotting carcasses of a hundred buffalo. The herd had been driven over the precipice by the Indians, who had taken all the meat they could carry and left the rest to the wolves and bears.

Day by day, the men toiled at the tow rope, wading waist deep in icy water. Their feet sank in mud, pulling off their moccasins, and their soles were cut as they scrambled over the rocky shores. The weary voyagers made camp on a point of land where the river forked into two almost equal channels. There was no signpost saying "This way to the Missouri."

The party must make a right choice if they were to reach the Pacific before winter. To the men, it was plain that the north fork was the right one. It was muddy and roiling and had the look and feel of the Missouri that they knew so well. Even Cruzatte the riverman was sure of it. The south fork was clear and deep, a mountain stream coming out of the West. The captains thought that this must be the main stream.

Just to make sure, each captain made an exploring trip up one of the forks. Lewis and six men went up the north fork. He came back after four days sure it was not the Missouri. This river went too far north. In the wind and the rain, he and some of the men had nearly slipped over a precipice. He named this stream Maria's River, after a girl in far-off Virginia.

When they got back, they found that Captain Clark had been anxiously awaiting them for two days. Clark had come back from his trip sure that the south branch was the true Missouri. Though the men were still certain the north fork was the Missouri, they were willing to follow wherever the captains led. Just to be safe, Lewis and some of the men went ahead up the south fork. If they found the great falls which the Indians had described to them, they would know they were on the Missouri and Lewis would send back word for the expedition to follow.

While the main body waited at the forks for news from Lewis, they decided to leave some of the baggage that would not be needed. The red pirogue was taken out of the water and lashed to a tree above flood level. They were leaving all the ammunition, provisions, and heavy luggage they could spare, to be picked up on the return trip. On a high dry spot Drewyer dug a small hole. As it went down, the hole was widened until at a depth of six or seven feet it was shaped like a teakettle. The dirt was taken out and thrown in the river. The goods were wrapped in skins and laid in this hole on a bed of dried sticks. When the sod was placed over it, no trace of the hole could be seen. This was called a *cache*. If it was not found by the noses of the wolves or the eyes of the Indians, the contents would keep in good condition for years.

The Falls of the Missouri: June 13, 1805

The first day out Lewis was taken seriously ill. He made himself a medicinal drink from boiled chokeberries. This brew was so bitter that a couple of draughts drove out the devil. Next day the party met two huge brown bears among the cottonwood and killed both with the first shots. Crossing a level prairie the following day, Lewis heard the distant thunder of falling water and saw a high column of mist rising in the sky. He climbed a range of hills and clambered down the face of the rock, his soft moccasins finding toeholds in the crevices. At the bottom, he stood breathlessly gazing through the drifting mist at the shining wall of the

great falls where the mighty Missouri plunged over an eighty-foot rock shelf in a long sheet of water more than a hundred yards wide. Its roar filled his ears with a deep and awful clamor. Over the water, in a prism of iridescent color, hung the shining arc of a perpetual rainbow. In the waters above was a pine-clad island. Here against the dark trees, an eagle perched above its nest on the top of a blasted pine trunk. The Indians had told Lewis that on this island above the falls the eagles had nested from time immemorial. Below the falls the waters rushed in mad swirls through a five-mile canyon, between steep walls of black rock.

A Day's Adventure: June 14, 1805

Following up the river above the falls, Lewis found a series of beautiful cascades that tumbled down over the rocky ledges. Farther on, the river flowed smoothly through a grassy plain filled with buffalo. Vast flocks of geese floated on the calm waters. And far beyond were the snow-capped mountains.

He fired at a buffalo and stood waiting for the wounded animal to drop. Something told him to look behind him. Within twenty paces was a huge grizzly walking toward him. In a flash his gun was at his shoulder—but he realized he had not reloaded. As the bear advanced, Lewis turned and started walking slowly toward the nearest tree, three hundred yards away. The bear, with a rumbling growl, charged, open-mouthed. Lewis raced for his life. The bear was gaining on him rapidly. He saw he could never make the tree. Turning sharply, he raced for the river. As he plunged in waist-deep, he turned, brandishing his spontoon. This weapon was a spear-ax or halberd, to which somehow he had held tightly during his sprint. The bear stopped short on the bank, swaying from one leg to the other. He was baffled. Lewis brandished the spear furiously and shouted, "Go home." The great beast wheeled around and ran off in a panic. Lewis climbed out, found his gun, and reloaded it. He swore never again to leave it unloaded.

He went on to explore along a river that ran into the Missouri. It must be the one the Indians had called the Medicine River. Along the bank ahead, he saw a strange creature that looked like a wolf. As he came nearer the creature crouched like a cat ready to spring. Lewis fired at sixty paces and the animal ran into its burrow. From the tracks and general appearance he "supposed it to be of the tiger kind."

It was six o'clock and time for striking back to camp. As he crossed the open prairie, three great black bulls broke away from the buffalo herd and came charging toward him with heads down. This time the captain, instead of running, coolly walked directly toward the charging bulls. He was certainly no toreador, but he simply could not see himself running from so stupid a beast as a buffalo bull. It was the bulls who stopped! They stood staring at him with rolling eyes from a distance of about a hundred paces. They were the lords of the prairie, but here was their master, and the strange man-smell filled them with terror. They tossed their heads, swung around, and galloped off.

It was dark and the camp was at least twelve miles away. But Lewis set his course by the stars and his compass and finally picked up the gleam of the campfire. The men were anxiously preparing to search for him in the morning. He ate ravenously and slept under the stars. When he opened his eyes next morning, they rested on a sight that brought him up with a start. Directly above his head a rattlesnake was coiled around the treetrunk under which he had been sleeping. He promptly killed it and wrote a minute description of its anatomy in his journal. The past twenty-four hours seemed a fantastic nightmare, crowded with bears, snakes, and buffalo bulls, with the majestic falls of the Missouri roaring and tumbling through it all; except for the thorns of the prickly pear in his moccasins it might have been a dream.

Portage: June 15 to July 15, 1805

Lewis had sent back word to the main party to come on. Clark pushed up the river to the foot of the rapids, where he camped, sending word to Lewis to rejoin him.

Sacajawea had been taken ill and could no longer walk. As Clark felt her feeble pulse, he wondered whether she could live. Lewis, coming back from the falls, tended her daily. Around the campfires, the men spoke in hushed voices, as they realized how much they valued and esteemed "the Indian woman." The crisis passed, the pain vanished, her strength and appetite began to come back. Again the men sang and danced around the fires. Sacajawea had pulled through.

Clark's party, with torn feet, advancing waist-deep in the icy water, had hauled the canoes "with undiminished cheerfulness" up the rapids to within five miles of the falls. As there was no way of going up the falls, they would have to take the boats around them. This made it necessary to cache such heavy items as the white pirogue and the swivel cannon. The carpenters sawed slices from the trunk of a cottonwood tree and made wheels for a carriage to haul the canoes around the falls. The hunters brought in enough meat for the trip from the vast buffalo herds on the opposite bank. The plains were black with buffalo. The hunters saw ten thousand in a single day. As the animals crowded down the steep banks to drink at the falls, scores were pushed into the rushing torrent by those behind and were drowned. On the shores below, wolves, bears, and eagles fed fat on their carcasses.

Clark made a survey of the portage and staked out the road. The sweating men hauled the canoes on the clumsy carriages or staggered on under their heavy baggage packs. In the broiling summer heat swarms of mosquitoes and gnats assailed their naked bodies. There were frequent stops for rest when the exhausted men dropped on the ground from fatigue. When a strong breeze sprang up, they hoisted sail on one of the canoes and the boat bowled over the prairie amid cheers. After supper those that could still stagger danced and sang to Cruzatte's music. The rest crawled under their mosquito nets and slept the dreamless sleep of exhaustion. "No one complains and they go on with cheerfulness," wrote the captains in their journal. The members of the expedition had hardened into a tough unbeatable team that took each day's fierce effort in a steady stride. They were determined to reach the Pacific or perish in the attempt.

After an eighteen-mile haul, the men dragged the canoes down to the river above the falls and made camp. Here they joined up the iron boat frame that had been lugged all the way from Harpers Ferry. The men sewed hides together and stretched them on the iron frame. In place of tar, they made a slimy mess of charcoal, beeswax, and buffalo tallow, and smeared it in the seams. When launched, the boat swam perfectly, but next day rough weather blew up, her seams opened, and she started to sink —a total loss. Nothing to do but build a couple of canoes to take her place. The men had to walk eight miles to find a couple of cracked and rotten trees of which to make two canoes.

Through the clear air, they could see to the north and west the white and glistening "shining mountains." From this direction, out of a cloudless sky, came strange noises like the explosions of cannons. No one knew their cause and so they called this mysterious sound the "mountain artillery."

Opposite the camp, on the White Bear Islands, the grizzlies were so numerous that no one dared to go there. At night raiding bears prowled around the camp while faithful Scannon barked fiercely every time a prowler drew near.

Finally the canoes were finished and loaded and the expedition resumed its toilsome way against the swift river current toward the ever-nearing Rockies.

A Close Call: June 20, 1805

Sacajawea was so much recovered that she and little Baptiste tagged along after Charbonneau and York as they marched upstream with Captain Clark, who was making notes for his map. They had gone some distance above the falls when wind and rain suddenly came upon them. "Better scurry up to that near ravine and take shelter under the rock shelf," Clark advised. There they squatted, cozy and dry, as the rain poured down. Soon the rain became blinding sheets of water; then it turned to driving hail. Looking up the deep gully, Clark saw an eight-foot wall of water rushing down the ravine, carrying trees, rocks, and everything before it. Shouting to Charbonneau, he grabbed up his gun and shot-pouch. Sacajawea had seized the baby, and Clark pushed her up the cliff ahead of him while the terrified Charbonneau hauled at her arm. Before they reached the top of the cliff, the water was up to Clark's waist and still rising. The stream had risen fifteen feet.

It was another close call. There had been many, but each time the captains had acted quickly and wisely, and disaster had passed them by. This time Clark had lost his compass and a cherished umbrella which he had persisted in carrying across the continent. Charbonneau's tomahawk and gun had gone over the falls, but the little squaw held her papoose safely to her breast. York, coming back from a buffalo hunt, found them.

When they returned to camp, the men were straggling in, bruised and bleeding; the wind-driven hailstones had knocked some of them down and bruised them all badly. The savage land had sudden and desperate surprises for the invaders of her ancient mysteries.

The Three Forks: July 25, 1805

From the White Bear Islands the canoes again advanced up the winding river. As the men toiled in the broiling heat, they glimpsed in the distance the cool snow-clad peaks of the Rocky Mountains. The hills closed in, forming two walls of rock that towered twelve hundred feet from the water's edge. "Nothing can be imagined more tremendous than the frowning darkness of these rocks which project over the river and menace our destruction." For five miles they continued through this majestic canyon, which they called "The Gates of the Rocky Mountains."

Farther on the country opened out into beautiful prairie surrounded on all sides by mountains. Through this country ran three rivers. They were called the three forks of the Missouri because at this point they joined to make the great Missouri River. No single one of these streams could be truly called the Missouri, so the captains named them separately after three great heroes of democracy: Jefferson, Madison, and Gallatin. Here all the Indian trails from over the mountains converged as they went down to the buffalo plains. For ages this had been a battleground between the eastern and western tribes. The men anxiously watched the shores for signs of Indians and carried American flags on the canoes to show that they were white men and friends.

The Shoshones had taken refuge in these barren mountains from their enemies, the fierce Sioux, who had obtained guns from the white traders. Here the Shoshones were forced to live in semi-starvation on roots and berries. Their only wealth was plenty of good horses. On these they ventured down to the plains in the autumn to hunt the buffalo. Their scouts had seen the strangers on the river and had sent up a smoke signal to warn their people.

Clark and three men had left the canoes before entering the Gates of the Rockies and had pushed overland to the Three Forks. Clark had gone on up the west fork for twelve miles. While overheated he drank deeply from an icy spring and became painfully ill. In spite of his sickness, on the way back to camp at the Three Forks he had pulled Charbonneau out of a swift mountain stream into which he had fallen. The Frenchman had almost been drowned in the strong current.

The river was rapidly becoming too shallow for navigation. They had no horses and had seen no Indians. Without guides and horses to carry their heavy baggage the expedition could not cross the mountains which lay before them. Lost here in the heart of the Rockies, their situation would be desperate with winter coming on. As Clark was still ill, it was decided that Lewis should push on until he found Indians and horses, if it took a month. Indeed he said he would not come back alive without them.

THE VANISHING SHOSHONES: THE CONTINENTAL DIVIDE, AUGUST 12-13, 1805

For three days Lewis's party followed an old Indian trail. Drewyer and Shields on each flank were to signal Lewis and McNeal in the center by waving their hats on their guns, if they found fresh tracks. Coming over a rise, Lewis saw a moving speck in the distance. Through his glass he could see a man riding bareback, carrying a bow and arrows. This must be a Shoshone at last. When the rider had got within about a mile he stopped. Lewis waved his blanket three times—the Indian peace sign. He dropped his gun, took some beads and a mirror from his pack, and walked slowly toward the Indian. Signaling Drewyer and Shields to halt, he pulled up his sleeves to show his white skin and went toward the Indian, holding out trinkets and calling "Ta-ba-bone," which Sacajawea had taught him meant "white man" in Shoshone. Just then Shields, who had not seen Lewis's signal, blundered forward. The Indian took fright, wheeled his horse, and dashed off into the underbrush. For some minutes, Lewis was furious with disappointment and scolded Shields for his stupidity. Their party followed the horseman's tracks all that day till they became lost.

Next morning they continued on the old Indian trail which they had been following toward a gap in the mountains. As the stream narrowed McNeal straddled it with his long legs, waved his flag, and shouted, "Thank God, I've lived to bestride the Missouri." They came to the place where the little brook welled up from the earth. This must be the very source of the Missouri. Here they rested, drank of the spring, and talked of their long adventure up the three thousand miles of river. They crossed through the gap in the mountains and on the steep downward slope found a westward flowing brook. This meant they had crossed the very backbone of the continent; here was water that flowed into the Columbia River and down to the Pacific Ocean.

Next morning they pushed on westward down the valley under a lofty mountain range. About a mile ahead of them they sighted figures. They could see a man, two women, and some dogs. Lewis put down his gun and advanced alone, waving an American flag. The Indians promptly disappeared, leaving only the dogs. Lewis tried in vain to catch one. He wanted to tie some beads around his neck and send him back to the Indians as a good-will messenger.

As they went on, the grass was trampled with the tracks of men and horses. They were close upon the Shoshones at last.

Coming suddenly out of a ravine, they surprised three Indian women. One ran but the other two—one an old woman, the other a child—dropped on their knees with their heads bent to receive the tomahawk of the enemy. Lewis gave them mirrors and beads, and painted their beaming faces with vermilion, a Shoshone emblem of peace. They all started toward the Indian camp.

Suddenly Lewis saw a sight that made his heart leap for joy—sixty Shoshone warriors riding at full speed, the dust billowing out behind them. They were magnificent riders on superb horses. Any Virginian could see that. The Indian bands pulled up their horses as the squaws held out their presents. Lewis put down his gun and came forward with his flag. Three chiefs leaped from their horses and ran up to give him "the Shoshone hug," putting their left arms over his right shoulder and rubbing their painted cheeks against his and shouting "Ah-hi-i, ah-hi-i," which meant "I am much pleased." The other braves followed. Sixty Shoshone hugs apiece had well greased the white men's faces with Indian paint, but Lewis was very happy. Chief Cameahwait rode into camp carrying the American flag, with Lewis following him, and the Shoshone warriors bringing up the rear.

Persuading the Shoshones: August 16, 1805

Lewis rose and faced the circle of sixty seated Shoshone warriors. They had pulled off their moccasins as a sign of good faith and friendship. The greenstone peace pipe had been passed around and all had smoked it. Behind them stood the women, children, and dogs gazing intently at the first white men they had ever seen.

Lewis was anxiously aware that the success of the whole expedition now depended on the effect of his words on these suspicious savages. He paused frequently as Drewyer translated in the dramatic pantomime of the Indian sign language. The white men had come to trade with the Indians. They brought the Indians guns, beads, knives, vermilion. They wished to cross the mountains and go to the great salt water beyond. If the tribe would return to the forks of the Jefferson with him, they would meet his brother chief with more white men who were being guided by a Shoshone woman, one of their own people. With them they would see a man whose skin was entirely black. The white men would trade many good things with the red men for their horses.

After the speech, the usual presents were distributed—beads, ribbons, looking glasses, and vermilion paint. The strangers had not eaten since yesterday. Would their red brothers oblige with some food? The Indians had only some cakes of dried berries. They shared the last of them with the strangers. Lewis asked Chief Cameahwait many questions about the westward mountain streams, but the chief was sure that they were too wild and rocky for canoes to pass. Lewis now looked carefully at the herds of fine horses that grazed about the camp. That night the weary white men watched the Indians dance till midnight and then slept with the drums of the dancers sounding through their dreams.

Lewis knew that Clark and his men were hauling their canoes up the shallow rapids of the Jefferson toward the Three Forks. Here he must meet them with horses and Indian guides if they were to cross the mountains before snow closed the passes. Cameahwait was friendly and willing to help but his warriors, who had recently suffered a terrible defeat in battle with their enemies, the Pah-kee or Minnetaree, were suspicious and gun shy with the strangers. Someone had circulated the unpleasant rumor that the white men were allies of their enemies and were planning to lead the Shoshones into a trap. Lewis repeated all the fine things the Indians would receive in trade for the horses. He was grieved the Indians could believe him so treacherous and false. They should know that the white men never lied. Were the Indians afraid to come and see if he spoke the truth? Were their warriors cowards? Were they afraid to die?

But only Cameahwait and six or eight of his warriors accompanied the party as they started back through the Lemhi pass toward the Forks amid the dismal wailing of the squaws. They had not gone far before a dozen more braves overtook them and soon the whole tribe had changed their minds and followed.

Before starting, the Indians had an antelope hunt but it had been a complete failure and they were now without food. Lewis and his men were down to their last pound of flour. An Indian scout came racing back with news that Drewyer, who was hunting ahead, had killed a deer. Lewis was carried along in the wild stampede of the tribe. He watched with disgust the Indians devour the raw entrails of the deer, which Drewyer had thrown aside. The Shoshones had been terribly hungry for a long time. They might have simply taken the whole deer by force, but the Indian code said, "To the hunter belongs the kill."

More deer were killed and by the time the party arrived within two miles of the Forks the ravenous Indians had gorged their fill. As yet there was no sign of Clark. The Indians were becoming very restless and increasingly suspicious of being ambushed. If the Shoshones should now bolt for the mountains, the whole expedition would be hopelessly abandoned in trackless country without horses or guides. Suppose Clark had not been able to get the canoes up the rapids? Lewis's anxiety increased, though he gave no outward sign of it. The Shoshones disguised the white men with furs and feathers, so that they looked like Indians. In case of an ambush, they would be taken for Shoshones by the enemy. In return Lewis placed his cocked hat and feather on Cameahwait's head as a token of his complete confidence. The two chiefs looked like figures in a masquerade.

As a last desperate token, Lewis gave the chief his gun, telling him "that he might shoot him as soon as they discovered themselves betrayed." The captain remembered the note he had left for Clark at the Forks, telling him which branch he had taken. He sent Drewyer to get it and explained to Cameahwait that it was from his brother chief, saying he was not far away.

That night Lewis laughed and joked among the uneasy Indians with a gaiety he did not feel. Through his dreams ran the uneasy refrain, "Can we hold them another day, if Clark does not come?" Before dawn Drewyer left camp with a note to Clark from Lewis saying hurry, hurry, hurry.

Meanwhile Clark and his exhausted men were sloshing through the icy waters of the Jefferson, dragging the canoes along the rattlesnake-infested rocks of its winding, shallow channel. From the top of a hill near where they had camped he could see the Forks only four miles away.

Next morning, Clark, Charbonneau, and Sacajawea walked alongshore, while the canoes followed the winding course of the river. Clark was amazed to see Sacajawea, who was in the lead, suddenly begin to leap and dance. To Clark it seemed that the sober little Indian woman had gone suddenly mad. She ran toward him, pointing and sucking her fingers, a Shoshone sign meaning, "These are my people." Riding toward them was a party of Shoshones, with Drewyer, in his Indian disguise, at their head. He quickly reported Lewis's whereabouts to Clark. The warriors now broke out into joyful chanting as they escorted the party to the Shoshone camp.

As the two companies met, a Shoshone woman ran forward and embraced Sacajawea. They had been taken captive together by the Minnetaree five years before, but she had escaped and returned to her people. Now others recognized Sacajawea and ran to greet her. The whole tribe was wild with excitement.

The captains clasped hands with a look in their eyes that said many things beyond words. They had never failed each other in the dangers and travail of all the long journey. Both were soon well smeared with grease from the Shoshone hugs. The beaming Cameahwait seated Clark on a white robe and placed on his head a crown of six precious seashells from the Pacific. He bestowed his own name on Clark, a ceremony which was an Indian token of enduring brotherhood. The council circle was formed; everyone took off his moccasins, and the peace pipe went around.

When the speechmaking was about to begin, Sacajawea was called to act as interpreter. She came forward and seated herself with her eyes on the ground. When it came her turn to speak, she looked up at Cameahwait. With a cry she leaped up and rushed into his arms, shaking with sobs. He was her own brother. She threw her blanket about them as they embraced and wept. When she sat down again and began to interpret, the tears kept coming and she stopped, to let them fall unashamed. After the council, she learned that all her family were dead, except two brothers and the little son of her oldest sister, whom she immediately adopted. Lewis had always considered the poker-faced squaw incapable of human feeling. He knew better now.

Good-by to the Missouri: August 17, 1805

The white men and the Shoshones camped together at the forks of the Jefferson on the barren backbone of the continent. Indian tribes from west of the Rockies were moving eastward toward the Missouri for the annual buffalo hunt. The white men were facing westward toward the jagged ranges they must scale to reach the Pacific before winter. They were not sorry to say good-by to the Missouri. Nevertheless, though they had fought against its winding snag-infested current for months, the river had always been a sure guide through unknown lands.

The expedition now split into two parties. Clark, with eleven men and three packhorses, crossed over the Lemhi pass and pushed on into the mountains, to seek a possible waterway to the Columbia. The river he was following rushed in churning rapids through ever wilder gorges, under towering cliffs, until it disappeared through a chasm in a distant snow-capped mountain range. After sending back word to Lewis, the party, very hungry and discouraged, turned back toward the Shoshone camp.

August 18 was a special day for Captain Lewis. That night he wrote in his journal:

> This day I completed my thirty-first year, and conceived that I had in all human probability now existed about half the period which I am to remain in this Sublunary world. I reflected that I had as yet done but little, very little, indeed, to further the happiness of the human race, or to advance the information of the succeeding generation. I viewed with regret the many hours I have spent in indolence, and now soarly feel the want of that information which those hours would have given me had they been judiciously expended, but since they are past and cannot be recalled, I dash from the gloomy thought, and resolve in future, to redouble my exertions and at least indeavour to promote those two primary objects of human existence, by giving them the aid of that portion of talents which nature and fortune have bestowed on me; or in future, to live *for mankind*, as I have heretofore lived *for myself*.

It was an odd and moody bit of autobiography to put into an official record. There was no one to talk to, as he looked forward and back on the lonely trail of his own thoughts. He could not know the dark fate he was so soon to meet, nor the long glory that would make bright his name. He wrote down his purposes in life and his determination to achieve them.

There was plenty of work at hand. The men sunk the canoes with heavy stones in the river, where they could be found on the return trip. All the excess luggage, including their anvil, they cached so that the Indians could not find it. But they treated the famished savages to an enormous fishfry from a catch of over five hundred delicious trout which they had seined out of the river.

Sacajawea learned that her brother Cameahwait had secretly ordered the Shoshones to start eastward the next day for the buffalo plains. She loyally brought the news to her white chief. The desertion of the Indians at that point would leave the expedition without horses or guides. Lewis immediately called in the Shoshone chiefs and accused them of breaking their solemn promises to him. Two of the chiefs said they had been against this but that Cameahwait had given the order.

There was a long pause. Cameahwait sat silently smoking his pipe. Behind an impassive mask, he was making a hard choice between his hungry people and his promise to the white strangers. Finally he said he had been wrong not to keep his promise. He would order the Indians to go back to the Shoshone camp with Lewis's party. Lewis wrote of the Shoshones in his journal:

> In their conduct toward ourselves, they were kind and obliging, and though on one occasion they seemed willing to neglect us, yet we scarcely knew how to blame the treatment by which we suffered, when we recollected how few civilized chiefs would have hazarded the comforts or the subsistance of their people for the sake of a few strangers.
>
> In their intercourse with strangers they are frank and communicative, in their dealings perfectly fair; nor have we

had during our stay with them any reason to suspect that the display of all our new and valuable wealth, has tempted them into a single act of dishonesty. While they have generally shared with us the little they possess, they have always abstained from begging anything from us.

After they reached the Shoshone camp, York and Cruzatte put everyone in a good humor with dancing and high jinks. In the bartering that followed, the captains secured twenty-nine fine horses. Cameahwait drew a map of the mountain country on the ground. An old Indian guide, who was sure of his way across the mountains, was engaged, with his four sons. "If Indian tribes with women and children can cross the mountains, we can do it," said the men to each other as they parted with the friendly Shoshones.

PART IV

Across the Rockies

Down the carved hills the bison come
To the cool wet buffalo wallows.
The monstrous bulls with dripping mane
Splash through the river shallows.
In the bottomlands the elk herd stands
And crops the flower-strewn grass.
By rushes rank along the bank
White swans swim slowly past.

Across the Bitteroot Mountains: From Lolo Creek to the Kooskooskee River, September 15 to October 7, 1805

The expedition was through with tow ropes and pole pushing. They now had twenty-nine horses for transportation through some of the roughest country in North America. The packsaddles were tightly cinched and the baggage carefully secured. The procession slowly piled up the slopes toward the snow-clad peaks that cut sharply against the green sky in long jagged ranges. They pushed through the thick brush and scrambled up steep slopes that became almost perpendicular walls. Sometimes a horse would slip and fall, rolling down the mountainside with his precious pack, to be hauled up again onto the rough trail. As they camped for the night, a cold rain turned to snow and then became sleet. Next morning they thawed out the frozen baggage and urged the weary horses over the steep snow-covered ridges.

Slipping and scrambling down a rocky mountainside, the explorers landed in a valley, where they came upon an Indian encampment. The Indians welcomed them by throwing their buffalo robes about their shoulders and willingly shared with them their own meager supplies of roots and berries. These Indians, who called themselves the Ootlashoots, were a tribe of the Tushepaw nation, and like most tribes of the western slopes, they were on their way east to the Three Forks of the Missouri and the buffalo. The tribe owned a herd of five hundred superb horses. There were speeches and presents and horse trading. The captains obtained thirteen fine horses from these Indians.

The expedition followed a rocky creek down a pine-clad valley and camped by a pleasant stream which they called "Traveller's Rest." That evening Colter came back from the hunt with three Indians. They were Flatheads and were in pursuit of two Shoshones who had stolen twenty-five of their horses. The Indians were given food and presents and invited to go with the party as guides. But they were close on the trail of their quarry and slipped off into the dark forests like pursuing wolves.

Farther on, the party came upon springs of boiling hot water that gushed out of the rocks. Here the deer and elk had worn trails and the Indians had dug a pit for a steam bath.

Foot by foot, they fought their way through the tangles of fallen timber and urged the crippled and jaded horses over the shoulders of bleak ridges. In the snowdrifts along the mountain-tops, for a while they lost the trail. Night after night the hunters came back empty-handed. The exhausted men shivered around the campfire, warming their half-frozen feet, and drank thin "portable soup" that Lewis had bought in Philadelphia. When the last of the corn and flour was gone, they killed and ate a colt. On the savage peaks that towered about them, it seemed that no living thing had existed for countless ages. Gaunt with hunger and weak with fatigue, the men grimly struggled on. They killed and devoured another colt and lived.

Again the captains decided to separate, as they had done in former emergencies. Clark, with six hunters, rode ahead, blazing the trail for Lewis to follow. As Clark's party advanced over the mountains the going became rougher. In a wild valley they shot a lone horse. That night the men gorged on horse steaks and left the rest of the carcass hung on a tree for Lewis's party to find. From a high ridge, Clark could glimpse a broad plain far to the west. With renewed hope they tackled the intervening ridges. Along the precipices, down ravines and creek bottoms, they struggled on through the foothills and out onto the plain. They were over the Rockies at last.

Clark's party had come down into the warm air of a plain that stretched westward. They hoped to find a way across this plain to the Columbia, the great waterway to the sea. Clark surprised three little Indian boys hiding in the grass and sent them off with presents to the nearby camp of their tribe. Soon the party was surrounded by crowds of wondering Indians, who fed the starved men with dried salmon and roots. Clark went in search of their chief, Twisted Hair, who had gone down the river on a fishing trip.

Lewis and his gaunt men followed Clark's trail-blazes across the savage wilderness. They found and feasted on the horsemeat Clark had left for them and rejoiced at the distant vision of the comforting plains. At last they struggled down through the tangled timber of the foothills to be met by the enervating warmth of the plains and the excited welcome of the Indians.

Lewis found Clark studying a map of the Columbia, which Twisted Hair had drawn for him on an antelope skin. The captains at once began to make their plans for reaching the river.

The Indians who swarmed out to marvel at the strangers from over the mountains were the Chopunnish, or Pierced Noses. The squaws brought baskets of quamash roots and dried salmon, and the famished men over-stuffed themselves with this unfamiliar food. Many were soon laid up with horrible bellyaches, and the heat of the plains after the cold and fatigue of the mountains seemed to drain the last of their strength. After a few days' rest, they began slowly to recover.

Their axmen felled five tall arborvitae trees and hollowed them out with fire and scrapers, Indian fashion, into dugout canoes. The men branded their thirty-eight horses and gave them in trust to Twisted Hair till their return. Their saddles were cached near the river. On October 7, they embarked in the five canoes on a stream which led to a river the Indians called the Kooskooskee. This stream, the Indians said, would take them to the Columbia.

Down the Columbia: October 7 to 17, 1805

The expedition was on the way again and the men in high spirits. "This is going to be easy," thought Sergeant Pat Gass as he shoved off in the last canoe. They were rivermen again, headed downstream to join the Columbia, in the five canoes loaded with their precious baggage, instruments, and ammunition.

They had been so used to fighting upstream and climbing over mountains that the first rapids of the racing Kooskooskee came as a surprise, even though Twisted Hair had pointed out such things on his map. A dozen times a day they came to places where the river rushed in wild swirls of foaming water down stream-beds filled with hidden rocks. The canoes raced through the boiling lather of white spray and came out safely into smooth water. There were places where the torrent was so violent that the captains and Cruzatte went ahead to study the current and to plan their course through the racing "chutes." Those who couldn't swim were put ashore, along with the most valuable baggage, which they packed on their backs. They were to join the canoes at the foot of the rapids. Sometimes a canoe hit a rock, tearing a hole in her bottom. The crew scrambled out on the rocks. Whatever floated was salvaged by the canoes downstream. There were many halts for repairs and drying out luggage.

The expedition reached the fabulous Columbia at last and the canoes pushed out into its broad current. Twenty feet down through the clear water they could see the armies of great silver salmon, coming up from the distant sea to spawn their eggs in the very spot where they had been hatched.

The tribes along the river caught the great fish and split and hung them on drying racks. Their flesh was then pounded into

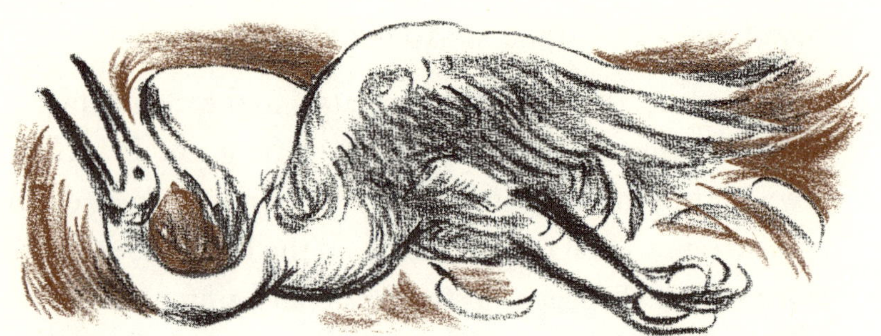

flakes, made into cakes, and packed neatly in baskets. These were buried, and in this way the fish would keep sweet for several years. What the buffalo was to the plains Indians, the salmon was to the Columbia tribes. The treeless shores of the Columbia were bare of game. Instead of the tender elks' tongue and buffalo hump of the Missouri, the companions now gagged on a tasteless diet of fish and roots. Once when they went ashore to purchase food from the Indians, two Frenchmen in the party, with more adventurous appetites, bought and ate a couple of Indian dogs. Other members of the party joined the dog-eaters' feast, until as many as forty Indian poodles were bought for the pot at one deal. Only Captain Clark disdained this delicacy.

They were now passing through the country of the Sokulk nation. These Indians were friendly and peaceable. The women were short and fat and their heads were flattened in such a manner that the forehead made a straight line from the nose to the crown of the head. A board was strapped over the babies' heads, so that this deformity was brought about painlessly as they grew.

Two friendly Chopunnish chiefs, Twisted Hair and Tetoh, had joined the party. As they pushed on down the Columbia these chiefs went ashore and made friends with the river tribes. The canoes were now making thirty to forty miles a day down the river toward the Great Falls of the Columbia.

Men from the Clouds

Clark quickly brought his rifle to his shoulder as the crane spread its great wings and rose from the opposite shore. There was a sharp report, a puff of smoke, and the bird fell with a heavy splash into the water. It would be sent to the President as a specimen. Clark was waiting for the four canoes to come down the river. As his canoe crossed the stream to pick up the bird, six Indians suddenly appeared along the shore. In a few moments they disappeared into the bushes. Clark could see the huts of an Indian village near the river. "Let us stop and smoke the peace pipe with them and let them know that more white strangers are coming," said Drewyer.

As the party came up the bank, they saw two or three Indians disappearing in the distance. Pipe in hand, Clark entered the low door of the first lodge. A group of perhaps thirty short stocky figures were crowded against the opposite wall, their black eyes filled with terror. Several children were crying and wild-eyed squaws were wringing their hands. He had never seen such fear.

The captain stepped forward smiling and took each Indian by the hand. He took some pieces of bright ribbon from his pocket and gave them to the squaws. As this seemed to have a favorable effect, the white men sat down. Clark took out his burning glass, and as the hut had no roof, he focused a ray of light on the pipe bowl. When the tobacco caught fire he took several puffs of smoke. Again a wave of terror swept over the savages and they drew back to the farthest corners. His efforts at friendship had failed. When he visited in the other huts, none of the Indians came forward to take the peace pipe from his outstretched hand.

At this point the main party arrived on the scene. The two Chopunnish chiefs explained the peaceful intentions of the party to the frightened Indians and pointed to Sacajawea with her baby. This assured the Indians that all was well, as they knew no war party ever took along women and babies.

Everyone joined in the sign-talk pantomime. Sacajawea told Clark that the Indians believed the strangers were gods who had fallen from the sky. The Indians said they knew this because they had seen it happen with their own eyes. They had heard a report of thunder, had seen the white crane fall from the clouds, and there before them stood the white god who brought fire from heaven to light his pipe!

Twisted Hair explained the object of the expedition and persuaded the tribe that the white strangers were only mortals who ate dogs, danced delightfully, and gave presents of gay ribbons and mirrors. The Indians then provided a supper of fish and roots; the peace pipe went around, and the white men continued on their way.

These practical Americans knew where they were going and with their rifles and axes they were going to get there in the shortest time possible. They were unconcerned with the meaning of savage superstitions. But in the ancient wisdom of the Indian, there existed an unseen reality and power behind all things. It was the Great Spirit who had given life to all his creatures and made them brethren. They saw his image in the beauty of lake and mountain and heard his voice in the wind and rain. He spoke to their wise men in dreams and visions. He heard their prayers and answered, when they danced the tribal dances for rain and harvest and victory over their enemies.

Nearing the Great Falls of the Columbia, the canoes passed under high black cliffs towering into fantastic shapes. Down their sheer faces, waterfalls spouted in long feathery banners of spray and mist. At the Falls the great river poured over a twenty-foot ledge. The canoes were unloaded and, with the help of the Indians and their horses, the boats and the luggage were portaged around the Falls and again put in the water. With long ropes of elkskin the canoes were eased down another drop of eight feet. At a place where the Indians had recently camped, the men made a new acquaintance—a multitude of fleas.

> These sagacious animals were so pleased to exchange the straw and fish skins in which they had been living, for some better residence, that we were soon covered with them, and during the portage the men were obliged to strip to the skin in order to brush them from their bodies.

These ferocious guests plagued the corps during their entire stay among the western Indians.

Below the Falls, the river opened out into a large basin. Here, directly across the river, rose a high black rock that seemed to block the channel completely. Clark climbed to the top and peered over. Far below they could see the river boiling through a rocky gorge. There was nothing for it but to "shoot" this narrow passage. The five canoes raced safely through, while the astonished Indians looked on from the top of the rock. Below this were more rapids, even worse. The nonswimmers got out and toted the valuables, while Cruzatte lashed the canoes in pairs and took them safely through the raging waters.

Next day they found that they would have to shoot another rapid that raced between high cliffs through a three-mile chasm "in which the water boils and swells in a tremendous manner." Again the valuables were portaged and one after another the five canoes shot through the wild rush of water.

After shooting these narrows, the party made camp on a high cliff which they called Fort Rock. The men repaired the canoes, picked off fleas, and entertained the visiting Indians with a dance to the violin. In the distance the white cone of Mount Hood rose into the blue-green sky. At this point the two Chopunnish chiefs, Tetoh and Twisted Hair, left the party and returned upriver on horseback.

Captain Clark went downstream to explore the next cascade between them and tidewater. The river bed was filled with huge rocks that might have been flung down by the angry gods of the mountains at the beginning of the world. Over these the river raced in rushing waves and whirlpools. Again there was the weary task of carrying the baggage over the slippery rocks and easing the empty canoes down the foaming cascades by means of poles. After two days of hard labor, they finally reloaded and rowed out on the placid surface of the river that now flowed untroubled to the sea. The weary captains wrote: "The rapid we have just passed is the last of all the descents of the Columbia."

To the Sea: November 2 to December 8, 1805

As the five canoes glided down the widening river, they passed a perpendicular rock that rose eight hundred feet above the water. They called this landmark Beacon Rock. Game was now plentiful along the wooded shore, where the Skilloot villagers came out to trade wappatoo roots for fish hooks.

In the river were large islands with ponds covered with cranes, swans, ducks, and geese, so numerous that their clamor through the night kept the tired voyagers awake. They met Indians in log canoes that were some fifty feet long and carried as many as thirty persons. These Indians wore the hats and jackets of European sailors and carried muskets and pistols which they said they got from the white sailors on the trading vessels that visited the Columbia. White fog and cold rain came in from the Pacific with a chill and bleak welcome.

One morning, as the sea fog lifted, the voyagers glimpsed a vast expanse of water that they thought could only be the ocean —"that ocean, the object of all our labors, the reward of all our anxieties." Faintly they could hear a muffled roar, the sound of distant breakers. The corps had come to the end of its long quest.

> This cheering view exhilarated the spirits of all the party, who were still more delighted on hearing the distant roar of the breakers.

The party pushed on and camped on a narrow beach under the high hills, in the drenching rain. A high wind rose out of the south, driving great breakers up the narrow shore. These waves hurled tree trunks six feet thick onto the shore as the men fought desperately to save the canoes from being smashed. From the cliffs above, rocks loosened by the rain came crashing down around the camp. Reloading the canoes, they tried to push on, but the wild sea was so dangerous that they were again forced to land. For six days they were pinned on a narrow beach by the raging storm that pounded the shore with enormous waves. The party lived miserably on dried fish and rain water. Clark had clambered up the steep slopes behind the camp only to find the forest wilderness barren of game. Shannon and Willard were sent

along the shore to explore the coast. When at last the wind fell they loaded the canoes, and, rounding a rocky point, came out on a fine stretch of beach. They were just in time to rescue Shannon and Willard. The two men had met some twenty Indians who had stolen their guns. When Lewis arrived an Indian was loading one of the stolen guns with evident intention of shooting the unarmed white men.

The weather-beaten party finally made camp above the tide water where they could see, through the clearing rain and mist, the waters of the Pacific to the vast line of its far horizon. They wondered at the passing Indians who managed their canoes so skillfully in the heavy seas.

The expedition had come to the ocean frontier, the final border of the western world. This was their mission accomplished. Now they must make new plans and important decisions. Behind them were the forest-clad mountains of Oregon. In the dripping twilight, under the trees, the hunters sought the vanishing elk. Above them towered the mighty trunks of trees two hundred feet high and twelve feet through.

The men sat around the campfire in the cold rain discussing future plans. Winter snows had blocked the mountain passes behind them. It was too late in the season to start back. They must find winter shelter in some location where there was game for food. The Indians told them that along the south shores of the bay there were herds of deer and elk. They decided to cross over and build another winter fort.

The expedition fought its way down the coast in the teeth of wind and rain and heavy seas. The roar of the pounding surf sounded continuously in their ears. Every day the hunters ranged back into the hills for elk. The men were sick of pounded fish and roots and yearned to sink their teeth once more into juicy red meat. For a few hours the sun broke through the clouds and John Shields brought in the first elk killed west of the Rockies. That night men feasted on elk tongue and marrow bones. The party camped on a narrow strip of sand and sat around the smoky fires waiting in the rain while Captain Lewis explored for a campsite. Lewis came back with good news. His party had bagged five deer and six elk and had found a site for the winter fort on the bank of a river across the bay. Slowly the canoes made their way against the wind and waves around Meriwether's Bay, which Clark had named after Lewis, and up the quiet river. The fort was laid out on a little knoll by a grove of giant pine trees.

Fort Clatsop: December 24, 1805

The woodcutters and the carpenters, under Sergeant Gass's direction, attacked the tall trees with axes and saws. It rained all day and every day. They worked in the rain. They ate in the rain. They slept in the rain. It came down in torrents, in sheets, in bucketfuls. It lashed in the wind; it drizzled in the heavy sea fog;

it trickled down their half-naked bodies and legs and swooshed in their rotten moccasins.

In three weeks the log fort stood foursquare. Its seven snug cabins faced one another across the fort yard. The outside walls of the cabins formed the stockade of the fort. The beautiful Oregon pine split into wide clean boards for puncheon floors and ceilings. Each room had a stone fireplace and chimney. The fort was named "Fort Clatsop" after the friendly Indians who were their neighbors. "Their chief Comowool is by far the most friendly and decent savage we have seen in this neighborhood," wrote Captain Lewis. The white men picked up enough of the Clatsop language to talk with the Indians. The Clatsops were very talkative, inquisitive, and intelligent. Although they were addicted to petty thieving and much gambling, and had armies of fleas, they had no appetite for the white man's whisky. They had flat heads and poor figures, but they held no resentments and kept the peace all winter. Lewis filled his journals with information about the Columbia tribes.

In spite of the rain and the fleas, December 25 was still Christmas. The celebration started at daybreak. The corps fired off every gun at once in front of the startled captains' cabins and then serenaded them with a Christmas carol. Then came the presents. The captains gave each other woollen socks and shirts and presented the men with six carrots of tobacco. Each of the men presented the captains with a remembrance. Sacajawea had been secretly preparing a surprise. She produced from nowhere two beautiful furs of ermine tails, one for each captain. The dinner was terrible—spoiled elk meat, fish and roots. But the spirit of Christmas shone brightly under the dark pine trees in little Fort Clatsop, four thousand miles beyond the Mississippi frontier.

Salt and Whale: Fort Clatsop, January 8, 1805

"Can you remember what salt tasted like?" said Shannon, chewing on a slab of leathery elk meat.

"Seems like I do have a faint recollection," replied Colter, grimly swallowing a mouthful of pounded fish. "I reckon a pinch of it would taste mighty good right now," he added.

A few days later, five men left the fort, heading for the coast. Each carried with his outfit a large iron kettle. They were going to set up a kitchen to boil salt from the seawater. A week later, two of them returned to the fort with a gallon of the precious salt, "white, fine, and very good." Keeping the kettles boiling day and night, they could produce as much as a gallon of salt a day. They also brought a strange kind of food the Indians had given them. It looked like fat pork and tasted remarkably like beaver. It was whale meat. The Killimucks had found the stranded carcass of a whale washed up on the beach. It was decided to send an expedition to procure some of this novel food. Sacajawea came to Clark with her black eyes flashing with excitement.

> The poor woman stated very earnestly that she had travelled a great way with us to see the great water, yet she had never been down to the coast, and now that the monstrous fish was also to be seen, it seemed hard that she should not be permitted to see neither the ocean, nor the whale. So reasonable a request could not be denied.

So wrote the good-natured Clark.

Next morning the expedition paddled down the winding creeks across the salt marshes and reached the long Pacific beaches where the salt boilers watched their fires. Here they found a young Indian who could guide them along the coast to the whale. Where there was no beach to follow, they must detour over a high promontory so steep that they had to pull themselves up a thousand feet of mountainside by clinging to the bushes. Seaward the fog hung like a thick white rug. As the fog lifted, Clark could see the long Pacific breakers fringing the white beach. Far below them they could faintly hear the seals barking where the surf broke on the black rocks. Sacajawea believed that the seal people were Indians who lived under the ocean. Over the void, a white gull wheeled with a shrill wail.

Clark stood in silence. So this was it. The last frontier. His mind went back over the long trail to the tall chief in the President's house, and, saluting, said, "Mission accomplished, sir. Your dream is an accomplished fact. The pathway of American destiny now lies open to the Pacific."

The fog lifted and they saw the gray sea stretching out to the long straight line of the horizon. Far up the beach they could see black specks that indicated the Killimuck village where the whale lay. "Go slow and careful," said the captain. "The ground is wet and slippery." Along the face of the barren hills the rains had washed hundreds of acres of clayey soil into the sea. The party followed along the edge of overhanging precipices that plunged into the sea and down the steep descent until they reached the beach below. Walking along the sand for two miles, they came upon the carcass of the great sea beast where it lay in the wash of the breakers. The Indians had stripped off the flesh so completely that only the huge skeleton was left. Captain Clark, always seeking for facts, measured its exact length—one hundred and five feet. Sacajawea walked up and down its vast length silently. On her back Baptiste snored softly.

The nearby Killimuck village was overflowing with whale blubber which the Indians were boiling down by means of heated rocks. Clark, by some hard bargaining, purchased three hundred pounds of the greasy food. Clambering back up the mountain, they overtook a procession of Indian squaws, bending under hundred-pound packs of whale blubber. One of them, trailing along the top of a cliff, slipped her pack, but she caught it and hung on to a bush with the other arm. Clark caught her as she hung over the edge and pulled her back to safety.

The party returned to the salt-makers' camp, where they had left their canoes. They paddled upstream on the incoming tide to Fort Clatsop, where hungry men waited for a feast of whale blubber.

Occasionally the Indians brought dried sturgeon and wappatoo roots to the fort. Once in a great while, an Indian appeared with the beautiful gleaming skin of a sea otter, the choicest of all the furs of the Pacific coast. The captains had just gone through the pompous ritual of bestowing medals on two Chinook chiefs who bore the exalted names of Comcommoly and Chillahlwil. Suddenly among the admiring crowd, their eyes caught the shimmer of sea otter.

> One of the Indians had a robe made of two sea otter skins, the fur of which was the most beautiful we had ever seen. The owner resisted every temptation to part with it, but at length could not resist the offer of a belt of blue beads which Charbono's wife wore around her waist.

She unclasped her precious belt of blue beads and held it out to Clark without a word.

GOOD-BY TO FORT CLATSOP: MARCH 23, 1806

Through the short winter days the men in Fort Clatsop made candles, jerked elk meat, dressed deerskins, made them into shirts, and fashioned several hundred moccasins. Each day the hunting party went for elk and deer. Day and night the sentinels paced the barrack's quadrangle and everyone who passed the gate was reported to the captains. At sundown all Indians were put out of the fort and the gates locked until sunrise.

The captains smoked and talked with the visiting Indians. Clark drew maps and Lewis wrote a long "general description of the beasts, birds and plants etc. found by the party in this expedition." He described at length the habits and appearance of the Indian tribes and wrote, "A Chinnook or Clatsop beauty in full attire, is one of the most disgusting objects in nature."

As the elk and deer moved back in the hills the rations at the fort became leaner, even though the Indians now brought in sturgeon and anchovies. All that was left of their trading goods could be put in two handkerchiefs. The party would have to depend on their guns for food on the homeward trip.

A paper was posted in the fort and distributed to the Indians, giving the names of the members of the expedition, its route, and the dates of their arrival and departure. The fort and all its furniture were presented to Chief Comowool in acknowledgment of his friendliness. The canoes were calked with mud. The hunters were sent ahead, the canoes were launched with every man in his place, and on March 23, 1806, in wind and rain they bade farewell to Fort Clatsop.

PART V

The Return

Oh, I've chawed on a lump of buffalo hump
and a beaver's tail from the bog
and I sometimes partake of venison steak,
but I never before ate dog.

CHORUS: Dog, dog, savory dog,
another helping of succulent dog,
savory and sweet, the beautiful meat
of delicious delicate dog.

I've eaten enough of horsemeat tough,
and rattlesnake steak and frog,
but all of my days I'll sing the praise
of a steaming stew of dog.

CHORUS: Dog, dog, savory dog, etc.

I've taken a chaw of liver raw
and the bark of a cottonwood log;
I've lived on roots and chewed old boots,
but give me a roasted dog.

CHORUS: Dog, dog, savory dog, etc.

Buffalo meat is fat and sweet,
washed down with water and grog,
but I'd much rather sup on a fat Indian pup
and another helping of dog.

CHORUS: Dog, dog, savory dog, etc.

Homeward Bound up the Columbia: From Fort Clatsop to the Kooskooskee, March 23 to May 1, 1806

The voyagers stabbed their paddles deftly into the water and pushed the canoes into the swollen current of the Columbia. The March winds roughened the surface of the river which the spring rains had brought to flood.

Day by day as the canoes slowly moved upstream they met small parties of Indians fishing for sturgeon and seal. Sometimes the party stopped for friendly trade and barter. They camped on Deer Island and hunted. The ponds and marshes were thick with geese, swans, cranes, and canvasback ducks. At night the frogs sent up a booming chorus and the banks swarmed with garter-snakes coiled up in wriggling balls. Wading in cold water to their armpits for hours, the patient squaws filled their canoes with the delicious white bulbs of wappatoo roots, which they dug from the muddy bottoms with their toes. Soon the multitudes of salmon would be rushing up the river, bringing plenty to the hungry tribes along its banks.

Half-starved families, coming down in their canoes from upriver to seek food in the lower valley, reported that above the falls as far as the Chopunnish nation the Indians were starving. There was no game on the plains and the Indians had used up their winter supplies of fish. At this news the party decided to halt and collect meat to last until they reached the friendly Chopunnish where they had left their horses on the trip west.

While the camp hunted and jerked deer and bear meat, Clark went exploring. Hidden from view by the river islands, he found the mouth of a great river which the Indians called Multnomah. It was later called the Willamette by the white men, who built the great city of Portland, Oregon, on its banks.

Clark stopped to visit a tribe living in a steep-roofed house built of boards. It was over two hundred feet long and divided into seven apartments. When Clark entered one of these, by the low hole that formed the door, the Indians drew back with sullen looks. They refused to smoke or trade, or even accept his offered hand. Then Captain Clark nonchalantly sat down before the fire, took a powder fuse from his pocket, broke off a piece, and tossed it into the fire. The flame flared up in a great sputtering blaze. The Indians shrank back in terror. A frightened squaw came forward, offering Clark a basket of roots. She begged him to quench the bad fire. As the blue flame died down he made passes with his hands to show his magic powers. The Indians now brought out more baskets of roots. Clark paid for what he took, made a few presents, smoked a friendly pipe, and returned to camp.

Again they loaded the canoes and paddled on under dark cliffs a thousand feet high. Down the rugged steeps little streams fell in long feathery ribbons. They again passed Beacon Rock and came to the foaming narrows. There they unloaded the canoes and carried the heavy baggage on their backs around the portage. A cold wind lashed the rain in their faces as they clambered over the slippery rocks. Lynx-eyed Indians hung about the piles of baggage, waiting for a chance to steal. The guards with short-barreled rifles stood ready to shoot anyone they caught pilfering. In spite of this, knives and hatchets continued to disappear at an alarming rate. In the rock-strewn river below, the men brought the empty canoes one by one up the furious rush of water with a single elkskin rope. It took three days to advance seven miles.

Reuben Fields had stopped and bought an especially tempting dog from two mean-looking Indians. When they found that he was alone, they attempted to take the dog away from him. Fields jerked out his long butcher knife and made a couple of slashes at his enemies. Terrified, they disappeared into the underbrush. Someone reported that Scannon, Lewis's dog, had been stolen by the Indians. Three hunters went immediately in pursuit with orders to shoot if there was the slightest resistance to returning the dog. Soon they heard Scannon's protesting barks and as the hunters came in sight the thieves "left the dog and made off." With a great barking and tail-wagging, Scannon was brought back in triumph.

While the main party was pushing up the Long Narrows toward the Falls, Clark traded among the Indian villages. With much difficulty he procured four horses at exorbitant prices. With the aid of these, they portaged around the Long Narrows and the Falls. From these thieving Indians Clark obtained six

more horses. Lewis furiously threatened to burn an entire village unless a stolen blanket was returned.

The baggage was now transferred to the backs of the horses and the canoes traded to the Indians. These Indian horses were wild and vicious stallions. In spite of all precautions some of them broke away each night. Precious morning hours were wasted in searching for them. The men were glad at last to leave behind them the chutes and rapids of the river and the thieving tribes that lived on its banks.

The captains engaged an honest Chopunnish Indian to guide them across the broken upland plains to the mountains and the country of his friendly tribe. At the end of a hard day's march the party halted to cook their meal of lean jerked elk meat. Suddenly a band of seven warriors rode up. The chief explained that he was Yellept, chief of the Wollawollahs, to whom the captains had given a medal last year as they came down the Columbia. He invited the white men to his camp. There they could rest and eat. He would give them plenty of horses. It was comforting to be again among friendly Indians.

At the Indian camp, the Wollawollahs provided plenty of fuel and fat dogs for the famished travelers. Yellept brought up a beautiful white horse that would delight the heart of any Kentuckian and presented it to Clark. In turn the captain gave the chief his sword, along with some powder and shot. The Indians brought them their sick for treatment. Clark applied salve to sores and eyewater to sore eyes, with healing effect. This resulted in more presents of dogs and horses. One hundred visiting Chimnapoos came that night for a big dance. Cruzatte played his gayest tunes and the men shook a limber leg. The Indians responded with their more solemn tribal dances. When the white men said good-by to their regretful Indian friends they had twenty-three fine horses. Three Wollawollah braves rode a day's journey after them to restore a steel trap that had been left behind. Lewis wrote in his journal:

> Of all the Indians whom we have met since leaving the United States, the Wollah Wollahs were the most hospitable, honest and sincere.

Recrossing the Mountains: May 1 to July 1, 1806

Leaving the hospitable Yellept, the explorers marched across the broken plains toward the foothills of the Rockies. It was a lean land and the Indian families they met were poor and hungry after a long winter. They found one of the Indian guides who had taken them down the Columbia. He said he would lead them to Twisted Hair, with whom they had left their horses and saddles the year before. They were anxious now to recover the horses for the journey across the Rockies, before the Indians left for the buffalo plains.

The Chopunnish lived in long shedlike houses that accommodated ten or more families. From them, the captains were able to purchase a few dogs, but these Indians, unlike many tribes, looked on dog-eating with contempt. As the white men sat at dinner one evening, an Indian who was watching them took a lean puppy and threw it into Captain Lewis's plate, laughing loudly at the joke. The enraged captain jumped up and hurled the unhappy pup in the Indian's face. Flourishing his tomahawk over the Indian's head, he said that he would kill him if he ever dared to repeat the insult. The terrified Indian departed and the dog-eaters finished their feast in peace.

Before them rose the peaks of the Rockies, white with snow. It would be another month, the Indians said, before the snow melted from the passes. When they reached Twisted Hair's camp they found the old chief in an angry mood. He was in the midst of a violent quarrel with Chief Cut Nose. The white men patiently listened to the dispute without understanding a word. The interpreter refused to interfere in what he said was a private quarrel and none of his business.

Drewyer finally persuaded Twisted Hair to smoke with the two white chiefs. After the pipe had gone round, the old chief calmed down. He said after his return he had cared for the horses of his white brothers; but Cut Nose had become jealous and so plagued him that he had allowed him to use the horses for hunting. Cut Nose had so abused them that their backs were sore, but as the horses were still in the neighborhood Twisted Hair would return them. True to his word, Twisted Hair rounded up twenty-three of the horses and recovered many of the saddles from the cache, where they had become somewhat damaged.

The captains gave the chief two guns and ammunition as a

reward. Clark treated several Indians for various ailments and they soon recovered. This news spread quickly among the tribes. He was surrounded by crowds of lame, halt, and blind men, women, and children begging for treatment. The captain patiently applied what simple remedies he knew and gave out eyewash. The trusting Indians came expecting to be healed and the treatments had marvelous results. Presents of horses and food were brought in by patients until the corps was again well fed.

As they advanced up the Kooskooskee River, visiting Indians poured in with presents of roots and dried salmon. A chief presented them with two horses, "without asking anything in return," and said that they might take any of his horses for food, "an act of liberal hospitality much greater than any we have witnessed since crossing the Rocky Mountains."

The captains held a council with seven chiefs of the Chopunnish at which they explained their proposals for universal peace among the Indians. This idea was accepted unanimously, although the speeches had to be translated into four languages before they were understood. The Indians guided them to a beautiful campsite by the river in a meadow lush with grass. Here they would await the melting of the mountain snows and prepare for their trip across.

For months Private Brannon had been so weak and painridden that he had not been able to stand. Someone suggested that he be given the "sweat bath treatment." As all else had failed, this treatment was applied. He was stripped naked and put in a four-foot pit that had been heated with a hot fire. The patient was covered over with a roof of willow poles and blankets. Water was then poured on the sides and bottom of the hole till the steam was as hot as he could possibly stand. After about twenty minutes, he was hauled out and soused a couple of times in the ice-cold mountain stream. This operation was repeated several times while he drank strong doses of "horse mint." This "robust" treatment so limbered up the patient that the next morning he was free from pain and very soon was as spry as ever.

The same day three Indians came in with an invalid chief. He had entirely lost the use of his limbs and had been completely helpless for three years. The amateur doctors thought the case hopeless. "Why not give him the sweat cure?" someone suggested. After the first application, he was able to use his hands and arms. When he was given another treatment he could move his toes and legs. In a few days he was healed. Captain Clark was now a very great medicine man among the Indians.

June had come. The spring was climbing out of the valleys up the mountainsides toward the white peaks. The river had subsided after the floods from the melting snows. The men at Camp Chopunnish were restless and anxious to tackle the mountains. The Indians said, "Wait till the next full moon when the snow has melted from the passes." To limber up, the men ran races, played prisoners' base, and danced with the Indians. The party now had collected a remuda of sixty-five strong horses.

On June 10, the caravan started toward the mountains in high spirits. Each man had two horses. They camped on a high plateau which they called Quamash Flats and next day rode into the heavily timbered hill country, over trails tangled with fallen trees. Higher up they came to great snowbanks ten feet deep, covering the rocks and fallen timber, but firm enough to support the horses. As the snow became deeper it completely obscured the trail. There was increasing danger of being "bewildered" in the trackless wilderness. Better go back while the horses were yet strong, to where they could find game and pasturage, and engage Indian guides who knew the trail. The heavy baggage, including their precious instruments and papers, was secured on high scaffolds. For the first time the expedition reluctantly turned back on the trail.

Drewyer and Shannon went ahead to the plains to secure guides among the Chopunnish Indians. For several days the main party slipped and slid down the mountainsides, the hunters searching in vain for game. At their old campsite at Quamash Flats, they met Drewyer and Shannon returning, with three Indian guides who knew the trail. It was one hundred and sixty miles across the mountains to Traveller's Rest.

The procession pushed its way into the gaunt world of snowy peaks to the mountain top where they had left their baggage. It was safe and untouched on the tall poles where they had left it. Their guides led them surely across the bleak ridges and along the tops of dizzy precipices. On the hard crust, where the snow had covered the rocks and fallen trees, the horses could make good time. The silent Indian guides moved across the wild landscape with a marvelous sureness. On the top of the highest peak, the party stopped to survey the panorama of desolation while their guides smoked to the Great Spirit. When they came to a southern slope where the snow had melted, they stopped and grazed their famished horses on the lush grass for half a day.

On June 29 they left mountain snows and rode down to cross the main branch of the Kooskooskee, climbed another high mountain, and camped that night at a spot where the hot springs gushed out from naked rock. Here everyone relaxed and took hot and cold baths to celebrate.

Next day the party made good time over an excellent trail.

There was plenty of game and the hunters killed six deer. They camped at Traveller's Rest Creek for a couple of days to rest the horses and to make their plans for the three-thousand-mile journey across the plains. The one hundred and fifty-six miles of Rocky Mountains had been crossed in six days. They would surely be back in St. Louis before winter. At Traveller's Rest the explorers made a bold decision. The party would separate. Lewis would proceed almost directly east to the falls of the Missouri and then explore northward along the Maria's River. If he were alive, he said, he would join the party coming down the Missouri at the mouth of the Maria's on August 5.

Clark was to go southward to the head of the Jefferson River where the canoes and baggage had been cached last year. Here Sergeant Ordway with nine men was to descend the river with the canoes. Clark, with the remaining ten men, including York and Charbonneau, and fifty horses, would cross overland from the Three Forks to the Yellowstone. They would proceed down this river by canoe to the Missouri, where, if they arrived first, they would wait for Lewis. Sergeant Ordway, with two men, was to go by land with the horses to the Mandan villages on the Missouri.

Distances and timing were carefully calculated and everyone was coolly confident that he would be at his assigned destination on time and according to plan. After two years of faultless cooperation, the captains and men counted on each other for perfect teamwork as a matter of course.

> All our preparations being completed, we saddled our horses, and the two parties who had been so long companions, now separated with an anxious hope of soon meeting, after each had accomplished the purpose of his destination.

WITH CLARK DOWN THE YELLOWSTONE: JULY 3 TO AUGUST 12, 1806

Captain Clark and his party started south from Traveller's Rest on July 3. Besides Clark, Sacajawea and the baby, there were twenty men and fifty horses.

They rode down a wide valley between snow-capped mountain ranges toward the Shoshone country where they would find the cache and the canoes they had left the year before at the forks of the Jefferson. Sacajawea guided them surely through the valleys and mountain passes she had known in her childhood.

At the Three Forks the soldiers rushed to the caches and dug up the twists of tobacco. They happily bit off huge mouthfuls. The men had not had a "chaw of tobacco" for months. The party proceeded with the canoes and horses down the familiar valley of the Jefferson. The land was teeming with game and at night they could hear the sharp slap of the beavers' tails on the water round the canoes.

At the Three Forks, where the Jefferson, Madison, and Gallatin joined to make the Missouri, the party again separated according to plan. Sergeant Ordway's party took the six canoes down the Missouri, and Captain Clark and his men, with Sacajawea and the horses, set out across the beautiful valley of the Gallatin, through Bozeman Pass and down the Yellowstone.

The great open valley of the Yellowstone was an Indian paradise where countless buffalo grazed. Sacajawea said that the colums of smoke they saw on the horizon were signals of the Crow Indians, a tribe of notorious horse thieves in whose hunting grounds they now were. Wild roses, luscious berries, and grapes grew thickly along the river bank. When the unshod hoofs of the horses became worn and tender, they were covered with moccasins of green buffalo hide.

Private Gibson fell on a sharp stick and badly wounded his thigh. He could no longer ride his horse. The party decided to build canoes and proceed by water. Trees were small and very scarce, but three axmen finally cut and hollowed two trunks to make a double canoe twenty-eight feet long, which would carry the party and baggage down stream. In the morning round-up of the horses twenty-four were missing. An Indian moccasin found near the camp indicated that the Crows had run off the horses. It was decided to send Sergeant Pryor and three men with the remaining horses across country to the Mandan villages to wait for the rest of the party to come down the Missouri.

They ferried the horses across the river, waved farewell to the sergeant and his men, and made sixty miles the first day down the swift current of the Yellowstone. Next day they stopped at a great flat-topped rock that rose two hundred feet above the plain. From its top, Clark viewed the wide sweep of the valley to the snow-capped Rockies on the horizon. Indians had cut figures of animals on the face of the rock. Clark carved with his hunting knife "William Clark, July 25, 1806." He christened the rock, "Pompey's Pillar," because the name sounded important and classical, and because Pompey was his pet name for Sacajawea's baby, who was not classical but very important, and of whom he had grown very fond.

Giant grizzlies along the banks rose on their hind legs to gaze, or swam fearlessly toward the strange invaders as they swept by in their canoes. From the canoe Clark shot two bighorns on the cliffs high above him. Great herds of almost tame elk fed along the river bottoms. Through the night the buffalo bulls pawed and bellowed. The canoe had to wait sometimes as much as an hour while the buffalo herds forded the river. The countless beaver people built their dams in the streams that wound through the valley. There were many rivers, the Big Horn, Little Big Horn, Windsor, La Biche, Table Creek, Little Wolf, Powder, and Tongue, flowing through this wild garden of unknown America to join the mighty Yellowstone.

On the lower river, they passed through the "bad lands," a

sun-baked region where the erosion of wind and rain had carved the colored earth into fantastic pinnacles and turrets. At last they camped and dried their baggage on a point of land where the two mighty rivers, the Yellowstone and the Missouri, joined. Clark figured that they had come eight hundred and thirty-seven miles down the Yellowstone to this point.

An enemy more fierce than bears and wolves now attacked the expedition. Day and night, clouds of mosquitoes tormented them. At night no one could sleep and by day the men could hardly work. Poor little Pompey's face was bitten and swollen. When Clark pointed his rifle at a bighorn the mosquitoes settled so thickly on the barrel that he could not take aim. He wrote a note to Lewis and tied it to a conspicuous tree where Lewis would be sure to see it. Slapping and swearing, the men loaded the canoes and the party pushed on down the Missouri.

"Look what's coming down the river," called the guard.

Two round bull boats pulled into shore and out jumped four men. It was Pryor and his party, with a story for the campfire.

Riding over the plains, they had been overtaken by a thunderstorm, and made camp, picketing the horses as usual. When they awoke next morning, not one of the horses was to be found. They followed the tracks of the Indian thieves for miles on foot. It was

impossible to overtake them. The miserable adventurers strapped their baggage on their backs and trudged gloomily toward the river, knowing that without horses in that vast and naked land they were in a bad fix. Coming out on the Yellowstone near Pompey's Pillar, Pryor suddenly remembered "bull boats." He had watched the Mandans on the Missouri making them from buffalo hide. He soon shot a great black bull and the men with their butcher knives deftly peeled off his shaggy hide. They made a round frame and stout ribs of willow rods on which they snugly secured the bull's hide with thongs, applying a final calking of buffalo fat. When launched, she floated light as a cork. Just to

make sure, in case of accidents, they made another. The party had come hundreds of miles down the rivers, two men in each boat, with baggage, without shipping a spoonful of water. The wilderness had its unpleasant surprises and desperate situations but by now the Corps of Discovery had learned the answers.

Clark's party continued slowly down the Missouri, daily expecting the arrival of Lewis. They met two trappers canoeing upstream. These were the first white men they had seen in over a year. The trappers had left Illinois about the same time as Clark and so had no recent news from the States. But they reported that the Indians at Fort Mandan who had so solemnly promised to make peace were now happily at war with their neighbors again.

"Here they come!" Every man dropped his work and ran to the river. Sure enough the six canoes were coming down the river. As the party drew near shore, they recognized all their companions except the captain. "Where is Captain Lewis?" demanded Clark anxiously as he pushed forward to the side of the lead canoe. Lewis smiled wanly at this friend from the bottom of the boat. He had been accidentally shot only the day before. He was suffering from a painful but not dangerous flesh wound. Clark knelt beside him and carefully dressed it. As the united party went downstream, Lewis told Captain Clark the story of his expedition on the Maria's River.

With Lewis to the Mouth of the Maria's River: July 3 to August 12, 1806

Lewis and his nine men rode eastward from Traveller's Rest toward the buffalo plains. Five faithful Indians who had guided them over the Rockies accompanied them for a couple of days to start them on the right trail and then turned back.

There was now plenty of game and as they came out on the plains they saw thousands of buffalo, whose bellowing filled the nights with a fearsome roar. Swarms of mosquitoes attacked till the horses became frantic and poor Scannon howled in pain. Grizzly bears rushed from thickets, but the hunters were afraid to shoot, as their Indian horses were unaccustomed to gunfire and might throw their riders. McNeal had knocked one huge grizzly over the nose with his gun and spent the rest of the day in a tree while the big bear waited for him to come down. Finally the great beast ambled off and McNeal overtook his companions.

On July 12 they reached the Missouri. Here they built two boats, Indian fashion, out of buffalo hide and crossed over to the White Bear Islands, where they had cached their baggage and left the famous iron canoe the year before. Lewis left Sergeant Gass with five men and four horses to portage the baggage around the falls when Ordway's party should arrive from the Three Forks.

From the Great Falls of the Missouri, Lewis with Drewyer and the Fields brothers, rode toward the Maria's River.

> The country here is spread into wide and level plains, swelling like the ocean, in which the view is uninterrupted by a single tree or shrub, and is diversified only by the moving herds of buffalo.

They were in the country of the vicious Minnetaree and the plundering Blackfeet and Drewyer kept a sharp lookout for Indian signs. As they approached the Maria's River, he picked up the bloody trail of a wounded buffalo. This probably meant that the Indians were not far away.

As they advanced up the Maria's, the weather became cold and rainy and the game very scarce. It was too cloudy to take celestial observations. It was time to turn back if they were going to make St. Louis before winter. Lewis called their last camp Disappointment and turned back next day toward the Missouri.

Drewyer had ridden ahead down the river valley. As Lewis rode up to the crest of the hill, his eyes caught something that made his pulse quicken. About a mile away he saw a herd of some thirty horses. With his spyglass he could see that half of them were saddled. On a knoll above stood a group of Indians, evidently absorbed in watching Drewyer in the valley below. The captain thought quickly. Should they run for it? But that would mean leaving Drewyer to the Indians. He had dealt with all kinds of Indians in the last two years, and he could negotiate with these. If there should be trouble—well, they were soldiers of the U.S. Army and trouble was their business. He explained his plan to the Fields brothers. They squinted their steel-gray eyes and nodded. They had followed the captains through tough spots before.

So they rode forward with the American flag fluttering gaily in the wind. They came to within a quarter mile before the Indians saw them. In a confused scramble, the redskins rounded up their horses and mounted. An Indian rode toward them. He stopped within a hundred paces, looked them over, and galloped back. As the whole band now came riding toward them at full speed, Lewis counted eight braves. Only two had guns; the rest carried bows and arrows. Fire power was in his favor. "Stand ready for attack!" he ordered.

But the Indians had halted and only one came forward. Lewis advanced and took his hand. He went on and shook hands with all the rest. He was now surrounded by excited Indians asking in sign language to smoke with the white men. Lewis was thinking how to reach Drewyer. "The white brave down by the river has our pipe. We must first send for him," said Lewis. When Drewyer arrived, the white men had four rifles to the Indians' two, and it was the Indians who were anxious. When three of them claimed to be Minnetaree chiefs, Lewis gave them a flag, a medal, and a red handkerchief. As the tension eased, he proposed that they all camp together by the river and spend the evening in talk.

Sitting round the fire, Drewyer translated in the quick gestures of Indian sign language, while the shadows of his moving hands flickered and danced on the high canyon walls. The Indians said they were part of a band that was hunting buffalo in the neighborhood. They did their trading with white men at a post six days' march away. Lewis told them of his journey up the great river to the big lake where the sun sets. Everywhere he had made peace among the Indians and had brought the good things the Indians desired. If his red brothers would come with their people to the mouth of the Maria's, there the white men would bring them many good things. But to this the Minnetarees made no reply. Each told an epic story of the wanderings of his people. The fire died down. Everyone was dozing off. When all were asleep, Lewis signed to Reuben Fields to stand guard. "If any Indian starts to leave, give the alarm," he whispered as he too stretched out between two sleeping Indians.

"Damn you, let go my gun!" The captain opened his eyes. In the gray dawn light, he saw Drewyer twisting his gun out of an Indian's grasp. Lewis grabbed for his rifle. It was gone. Every man around the fire went into action. Lewis drew his pistol and started after the redskin who was running off with his gun. "Drop that gun or I'll kill you!" he shouted. An Indian slipped behind Joe Fields and snatched up the brothers' rifles. They jumped up together and raced after him. As Joe grabbed the redskin, Reuben sank his knife in his side. The Indian staggered on a dozen paces and fell dead. Drewyer and the Fields with their recovered guns now ran to where Lewis stood pointing his pistol at the Indian who was slowly laying the stolen rifle on the ground. As the three soldiers raised their guns to fire, Lewis shouted, "Don't shoot. He can't do any harm now."

On the way back to camp, they saw four Indians driving off their horses on the other side of the river. Lewis ordered his men to pursue. They must recover the horses even if they had to shoot to kill. Lewis now ran after the Indian who had stolen his gun. Together with another Indian he was running off with Lewis's horse. As Lewis raised his gun, one of the Indians jumped behind a rock, calling to his companion. Lewis fired. The Indian fell, shot through the belly, rolled over, and fired from his elbow, grazing Lewis's head. Lewis, who had no more ammunition, started toward camp, meeting Drewyer who had run up on hearing the shooting to assist the captain. The Fields brothers now came back with four horses which they had recovered.

The white men quickly gathered up the Indians' bows, arrows, and shields as trophies, saddled their horses and rode off, leaving the two dead Indians where they lay, staring up at the morning sky. Around the neck of the Indian Lewis had shot was a peace medal with the bronze head of Jefferson on one side and the two handclasps on the other.

Lewis was sure the main party of Minnetarees would immediately try to head them off at the mouth of the Maria's. He must get there first, and meet the canoe party coming down the Missouri. Their horses were excellent and the ground firm and level. Hour after hour they rode steadily on. By three o'clock Lewis figured they had covered sixty-three miles. They stopped to rest the jaded horses and then rode on. As darkness came on, Drewyer shot a buffalo and they halted for a brief supper.

The moon shone through ragged clouds as they rode on amid the drowsing buffalo herds that seemed like ghosts in a dream of some lost world. By two o'clock that night they were utterly exhausted and slept in their tracks. At dawn they crawled stiffly from their blankets, mounted, and urged their jaded horses on.

As they were nearing the river, Lewis thought he heard the sound of distant firing. Were the Minnetarees attacking the canoe party? They spurred on faster. Again they heard firing, this time loud and distinct.

They dashed up to the top of the river bluffs and looked down with a great surge of joy. There below them in the river were the canoes and the old white pirogue. Sergeant Ordway was waving his hat and nearly going overboard with delight. They recognized the familar faces of their companions as the canoes came to shore. The two parties had reached the appointed rendezvous at exactly the same moment!

On the point of land where the two rivers met, the men opened up their last year's cache and took whatever was still undamaged. The red pirogue which they had tied up on the island last year was cracked and rotted past all repairing. Before they left, Sergeant Gass and huge lumbering Willard came in with the horses which they had brought down from the Falls on time and according to plan. The party had no more use for horses and turned them loose on the prairie. Even the drenching rains could not dampen the men's high spirits as the canoes went racing down the flooded river at seven miles an hour. Along the cliffs and shores, the hunters found abundance of game and the party feasted again on buffalo, elk, and bighorn. High in the sky soared the great calumet eagle and among the flocks of geese paddling alongshore they saw a lonely pelican. The hunters bagged a monstrous grizzly which measured nine feet from his nose to his tail.

The flooded river raced like a wild horse, carrying them past the mouths of the Musselshell and Porcupine, the Martin and the Martha and the Milk, all pouring sand and mud into the Missouri until the river water was undrinkable. The party made

eighty-three miles in one day, and on the seventh of August reached the mouth of the Yellowstone where they found Clark's note telling them he had gone by and was waiting downriver.

Lewis's party camped to calk the leaks and cracks in the canoes and to dry out the rain-soaked baggage. Their ragged deerskin clothes were almost falling off their backs. The men took needles and thread from their kits and made new shirts, leggings, and moccasins from fresh skins. They were only twenty-two hundred miles from home and they must be neat and smart on arrival.

Lewis had planned to reach a point known as the Burnt Hills by noon, in order to take observations, but they arrived twenty minutes too late. His disappointment was quickly forgotten when he sighted a herd of fat elk grazing along a willow bar. He and Cruzatte went ashore and each shot an elk. Reloading, they plunged into the underbrush for another shot. Just as Lewis was sighting his gun at an elk, a shot rang out, and he felt a burning pain in his hip. He had been shot through the thigh. Thinking that Cruzatte, whose eyesight was bad, had mistaken him in his brown leather jacket for an elk, he called out his name. No answer. Then it must be Indians. He limped back to the canoes calling for Cruzatte to follow him. Here he ordered the men to arm and follow him back to find Cruzatte. As he hobbled forward his wound became so painful that he had to turn back to the canoes. In twenty minutes the men returned with the crestfallen Cruzatte. The bullet taken from Lewis's wound fitted Cruzatte's rifle. It was apparent that he had accidentally shot his captain in the seat of the pants. "As Cruzatte had always conducted himself with propriety, no further notice was taken of it," Lewis wrote in his journal. They dressed the wound as best they could and made the captain as comfortable as possible in the bottom of the boat. Here he wrote in the journal, "As writing in my present situation is extremely painful to me, I shall desist until I recover and leave to my friend Captain C. the continuation of our journal." The party had met the two Illinois traders who had seen Clark the day before.

There was great rejoicing when the hunters Colter and Collins, who had been missing nine days, came into camp. The canoes pushed swiftly on "till at one o'clock we joined our friends and companions under Captain Clark."

The Last Stretch: Fort Mandan to St. Louis, August 14 to September 23, 1806

With the wind astern and paddles flashing, they had made eighty-six miles in one day. On August 14, they sighted the rounded lodges of the Mandans and Minnetarees atop the river bluffs. Below them the shore was soon crowded with excited braves, squaws, children, and dogs.

For three days they stopped among the hospitable Indians. While Lewis was recovering, Clark did the honors among the chieftains. He visited with the Black Cat, the Big White, the

Black Crow, and the gigantic one-eyed Le Borgne. The chiefs again promised to make peace with the Ricara but said they must defend themselves against the attacks of the Sioux. Clark urged the chiefs to come to Washington to visit their White Father. They were reluctant and offered excuses. All declined except the Big White. He said he and his family would come. As a grand farewell gift, Clark brought the swivel gun ashore and presented it, loaded, to Le Borgne in the presence of all the chiefs. The captain said he hoped that whenever it was fired, the chief would remember his white brothers and the wise councils of his Great White Father. "The gun was then discharged and Le Borgne had it conveyed in great pomp to his village. The council was then adjourned."

The captains urged Charbonneau and Sacajawea to come with them to the States but the trapper refused. He deeply distrusted the ways of civilization. He preferred the Indian life he knew so well and the freedom of the vast plains. So he was paid off in a lump sum of $500.13. Clark took Pompey, his "little dancing boy," in his arms for a last farewell. He had urged Sacajawea to let him take the child to St. Louis and educate him as his own son, but Sacajawea refused to give up her chief treasure. He was too young to leave his mother, she said.

Sacajawea was only a squaw and so received nothing. She said a brief farewell to her captains and stepped out of the story to resume her anonymous place in the life of her tribe. The silent little squaw had patiently toted her baby on her back up rivers and over mountains, guiding and leading, sharing the hunger, cold, and danger without complaint, always to be counted on, asking nothing except to see the great fish and the big salt lake; unrewarded, unforgotten, of courage undaunted.

The soldiers were now eager to get back to the States, to home and all the comforts of the white man's world. All except Colter. He applied for an honorable discharge from the army. He wanted to go back with the two trappers to the buffalo and beaver country. He had been a brave soldier and a loyal companion. If the men agreed, the captains would give him his discharge. The Corps all consented, wished him success, gave him presents and three rousing cheers, as he turned back up the river to a life of incredible and lonely adventure in the wilderness; but his homesick companions could not understand why "he should give up all these delightful prospects and go back without the least reluctance to the solitude of the woods."

As the expedition continued downstream, Captain Clark stopped for a last look at old Fort Mandan. It had been destroyed by an accidental fire and only a few charred logs remained. He remembered that here they had fought and won their first battle with cold and hunger on the edge of the unknown.

Farther down the river they passed through the Sioux country with their guns loaded, ready for a brush with these surly savages. They met only a few Teton stragglers with whom they exchanged insults and paddled on. The plains were black with buffalo—as many as twenty thousand, Clark estimated. As the canoes neared the Platte the party stopped to climb the bluffs, where they stood reverently beside Sergeant Floyd's grave.

Every stroke of the paddles was bringing them nearer home. Some days they made sixty or seventy miles, where they had dragged the barge wearily upstream only twenty miles a day. They now met small parties of trappers canoeing up the river to hunt and trade with the Indians. They asked eager questions and listened hungrily to the news from the States that they had not

heard for two years. Along the frontier and back in the eastern cities the expedition had long been given up for lost by all except the President. Now its members had suddenly come back from the dead. Their magnificent adventure had been accomplished. They had charted the path of American destiny across the continent. Suddenly they realized that they themselves were the biggest news in all the States.

A wild yell broke from the crew when they first sighted a yellow cow along the shores. They had come to fenced fields, farms, and now frame houses straggling along a village street. There was an exuberant welcome in the frontier villages where they went ashore. In the stores people bought and sold goods for bright silver dollars instead of fish hooks and beads. It was all a little strange and yet delightfully familiar.

They quickened the strokes of their paddles as they raced out of the Missouri into the Mississippi and down toward St. Louis, "where we arrived at twelve o'clock, and having fired a salute, went on shore and received the heartiest and most hospitable welcome from the whole village."

When the bronzed and bearded heroes in their ragged elkskins were paid off, most of them bought new store clothes, shaved, danced again with golden-haired, white-skinned girls, and in time married their sweethearts, settled down on government land granted to them by Congress, and raised large, towheaded families.

Gradually the everyday pattern of civilized living became reality and the eight thousand miles of wilderness, the long battle with the endless river, the bitter mountain passes, and the Pacific breakers in the rain became a slowly fading dream. The gaudy Indian villages, the painted warriors, the savage dances, the charging buffalo herds, and the wild riders became memory pictures relived in the firelight as wide-eyed children listened in rapture to a grandfather's tales on a winter's night.

Report to the President

The first morning after their arrival, Lewis rose early and wrote a letter to the President announcing their arrival and giving a brief and precise account of all that had happened since they had left Fort Mandan. He sent it by Drewyer to overtake the eastbound mail that was waiting at Kahokia, Illinois, for this official letter.

The captains now dried out the baggage and stored the furs and specimens ready for shipment to the President at Washington. They sat down together and began at once to copy out their field journals in neat little notebooks with red leather covers. The original pages had been written wearily by river campfires or on snow banks amid mountain peaks, on mosquito-infested islands and in the rain-soaked forests of Oregon. The record was a woven tapestry of word pictures of savage men and beasts, fishes, insects, and plants. It was a moving picture of toiling marchers through eight thousand miles of wilderness during the winters and summers of over two years.

In due course, through Mr. Jefferson's efforts, the journals were edited and the spelling corrected by Mr. Biddle of Philadelphia and they were published in three volumes which did not sell very well. The original journals lay forgotten for a hundred years in the library of the American Theosophical Society before they were printed for the first time, word for word, with spelling and grammar just as they had been written.

Mr. Jefferson pushed aside a pile of correspondence and swiftly scanned Lewis's letter. They were all safe, thank God. The thing was accomplished according to plan, only more splendidly and more daringly than he had hoped. In his long life he had made many dreams come true. This was one of them. The Republic would now extend from ocean to ocean. He reread the pages slowly, richly savoring the words, weighing the implications and overtones of the lean, brief statements.

The letter began:

> St. Louis, September 23rd, 1806
>
> Sir: It is with pleasure that I announce to you the safe arrival of myself and party at this place with our papers and baggage. No accident has deprived us of a single member of our party since I last wrote you from the Mandans in April, 1805. In obedience to your order we have penetrated the Continent of North America to the Pacific Ocean and sufficiently explored the interior of the country to affirm that we have discovered the most practicable communication which does exist across the continent by means of the navigable branches of the Missouri and Columbia rivers. . . .

The President paused and his eyes lifted from the page and out through the tall south windows across the Potomac to the Virginia hills, golden in the autumn haze. He was a connoisseur of men, and those two young Virginians whom he had chosen were the choice vintage of the living vine, the first fruits of the Republic. They were the first but not the last of a long line of pathfinders of the West. They were samples of the true breed, of what the new nation could be and do; he could trust the future to such as these. . . .

OF COURAGE UNDAUNTED . . . HONEST, DISINTERESTED, LIBERAL, OF SOUND UNDERSTANDING AND A FIDELITY TO TRUTH SO SCRUPULOUS, THAT WHATEVER HE SHOULD REPORT WOULD BE AS CERTAIN AS SEEN BY OURSELVES; WITH ALL THESE QUALIFICATIONS, AS IF SELECTED AND IMPLANTED BY NATURE IN ONE BODY FOR THIS EXPRESS PURPOSE, I COULD HAVE NO HESITATION IN ENTRUSTING THE ENTERPRISE TO HIM.

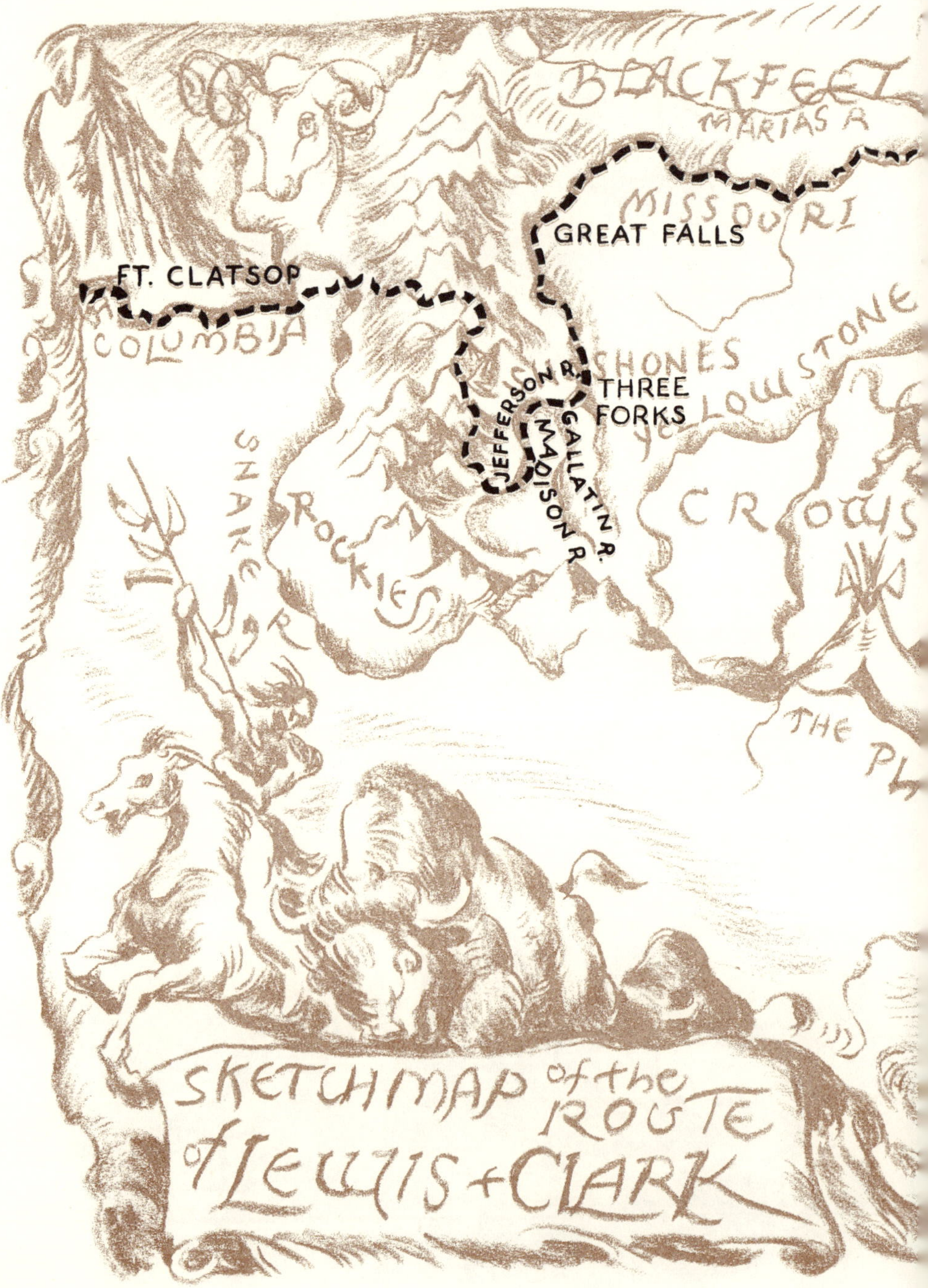
BLACKFEET
MARIAS R
MISSOURI
GREAT FALLS
FT. CLATSOP
COLUMBIA
YELLOWSTONE
SHONES
JEFFERSON R.
THREE FORKS
MADISON R.
GALLATIN R.
SNAKE R
ROCKIES
CROWS
THE PL
SKETCHMAP of the ROUTE of LEWIS + CLARK

MINATREE
FT. MANDAN
MANDAN
ARIKARAS
ARICARA'S VILLAGES
SIOUX
FLOYD'S GRAVE
BLACKBIRD HILL
COUNCIL BLUFFS
OTOES + MISSOURI
ST. CHARLES
ST. LOUIS

Brief Itinerary of Lewis and Clark[1]

DATE		PLACE	MILES
May 14	1804	Left mouth of Missouri River	0
June 26	1804	At mouth of Kansas River	340
July 21	1804	At mouth of Platte River	600
July 30	1804	At Council Bluffs	650
August 21	1804	At Sioux City, Iowa	850
Sept. 20	1804	At Big Bend of Missouri River	1,172
Nov. 2	1804	Arrived at Fort Mandan	1,600
April 7	1805	Left Fort Mandan	1,600
April 26	1805	At mouth of Yellowstone River	1,880
June 2	1805	At mouth of Maria's River	2,521
June 16	1805	At Great Falls, Mont.	2,575
June 18	1805	At White Bear Islands	2,595
July 25	1805	At Three Forks of Missouri River	[none recorded]
August 12	1805	At headwaters of Missouri River	3,096
Sept. 9	1805	At mouth of Lolo Creek	3,338
Oct. 10	1805	At mouth of Clearwater River	3,567
Oct. 16	1805	At mouth of Snake River	3,721
Oct. 22	1805	At Great Falls of Columbia River	3,873
Oct. 30	1805	At Cascades of Columbia River	3,944
Dec. 7	1805	Arrived at Fort Clatsop	4,135

[1]From *The Trail of Lewis and Clark* by Olin D. Wheeler, courtesy G. P. Putnam's Sons.

Index